CALLIOPE'S BOY

Tom Bradley

CONTENTS

Calliope's Boy

Having lifted up his lyre, he tried his song.
He sang that Earth, Heaven and Sea
were fitted together into one form,
and separated through Hate.
Apollonius Rhodius, *Argonautica*, I. 494

He looked like an aged pear with his olive drab raincoat stretched about him. He laid his instrument horizontally across the topmost roll of his gut, on a plane nearly a foot higher than the tops of many of the heads filing by. He arched his back, clenched his great soft buttocks, bopped his skull arhythmically against the hard curve of the ceiling, and didn't sing, but wheezed and grunted unconsciously, providing authentic-sounding mouth flatulence, in strict time, in order to exploit the bathroom acoustics of this yellow-tile tube.

Or else sometimes he did sing, three-four and whiny, the Pat Sky song that made America famous:

Our baby died last night.
It lived not forty-eight hours,
and it cost a hundred dollars.
It was a lousy baby anyway.

It died just to spite us,
of spinal meningitis—
wat 'n data ya-ga (forgot the words)
It was a lou-u-usy baby anyway-y-y.

Someone small and haunted-looking came by to sprinkle old ha'pennies like cinnamon powder into his case; and he leaned his huge head back in acknowledgement, letting this benefactor see the rich black soot which lined his nostrils now, identifying him as a bona-fide people's musician.

The same rough iron soot was accumulating on the skin head of his instrument, gradually making it, too, look more appropriate. Underneath all that authentic soot was a fabulous banjo, an Epiphone, custom-made extra large and fine especially for Sam. It was eight hundred dollars, much better quality than any other busker's instrument (poor slobs), and he flaunted it high upon his gut. It had been a present from his mom on his tenth birthday, way back in his boyhood's America.

In one of her quasi-fugue states she had taken him to a franchised music store where they mostly sold Magnavox Home Entertainment Centers. Strung along one wall in the back had been a few shiny trumpets and clarinets. And that's where Mrs. Edwine had led her Sammy, wanting to provide him with the mollification of playing beautiful music with his mouth.

After ten years she still had fresh in mind the sad hours she'd spent nursing her huge, lipless infant through a syringe, shedding tears because Nature had deprived her boy of the one activity which babies love most. And, of course, in her view, she'd been partly responsible: she'd helped Nature along by allowing gestation to take place downwind of nuclear testing sites. Unworthy is what Sam's mom sometimes felt in certain moods: generalized unworthiness. Sammy was her only weak point, and music her only field of ignorance.

So, on birthday number ten, after swinging by the credit union, Mom had yielded to the authority of the half-asleep sales clerk behind the wind instrument counter. She inquired, if her boy could have his pick of any he wanted, what instrument would best suit Sammy's double harelip (repaired)?

The clerk, evidently hung over, had looked slowly up and down at the six foot-tall child delivered up before him, and had mumbled, "Banjo."

If banjo it was, then fabulous banjo it had to be: customized with inappropriate mother-of-pearl squiggles and squirrels all up and down everywhere, and real secret Freemason symbols on the neck. It was physically painful to look at, it was so beautiful. Nevertheless, part of the obligatory game had been for Sam to pretend all these fifteen years that he hated his banjo. He'd left it behind at home. A cousin had secretly shipped it to him once he'd gotten situated at Herne Hill in unfashionable and perilous Brixton.

Somehow, from the way he made his banjo ring through the yellow tile tunnels of London's underground transit system, it was evident that this was exactly where this music belonged, as it were, and Samuel Edwine with it, evident that he'd taught himself to think and to feel and to play inextricably, all at once, down inside of another, similar place underground.

In a basement dug in a salt desert somewhere remote, pipes and heating ducts dangling like stalactites overhead. On a street called

Dimple Dell Drive, where he'd spent his formative years lying flat on his back, staring up at the ceiling, and thinking persecution thoughts about the polygamist cultists who surrounded him.

And now he did not fail to notice the secret undergarments of the Church of Jesus Christ of Latter-Day-Saints. It seemed, to his curdled corneas, that more than two thirds of his passing audience wore them, showing white and peculiar through the fabric of their dresses and shirts. London, as far as he was able to ascertain, was becoming a city of Mormon converts.

They wore the stretchy see-through things against their bodies, the original design, right down to the hamstring-gash still bestowed by fundamentalist overseas branches of the faith as a reminder of the things Moloch has in store for his Moronic Myrmidons who fail to bend their knees in submission and prayer. Yes, even through the thick tweeds, one's corneas could plainly see that the limeys' long-legged garments had slits in back, brown with dried femoral blood.

One could see why these lapsed Anglicans, each of whom took pains definitely not to gawk at him, must hanker, deep in their sunless souls, for a shot of New World zeal to jump-start their polite lives. And, of course, recent converts are always orthodox in their approach to the newly embraced delusion. They surely declined to remove their official garments, even keeping them hanging from one toe while procreating more pallid islanders; for the Prophet Father Brigham Young had long ago warned his children that it might be fatal to remove them completely under any circumstances.

They provide prophylaxis from the infections of the Devil; and true Mormons not only fuck and suck, but shower and swim and patronize Turkish baths with these gauzy eye-catchers swathed around them. These conspicuously pious whole-body scum-bags have pin-holes over each nipple so the soul may exit upon death or baptism by proxy, not unlike those poked with sewing needles in cellophane-packaged Trojans by counter help at Mini Marts all across the Far West, and beyond.

When Sam saw this salt-color glowing under the clothes of the sons and daughters of the thunderous Thames, he realized something about the ubiquity of cultural and moral and political and religious and sexual and aesthetic compromise. It was something so big and sweeping that he couldn't come close to articulating it, not even in the reasonably manic mood he was in these days.

So he decided to pack up his banjo and withdraw, to take a bath, for he felt besmirched with compromise. It would be his first and last bath this side of the Atlantic.

* * * *

He went to one or another of the bohemian parts of town, paid his few shillings, and was issued a stiff white towel, sandpapery with spider legs, and a virtually hairless slab of gristly soap. He could hear the moans of aged Cockney drunks drying out in adjacent booths, bums all around, singing sea chanteys like unshaven privateers.

He more or less stretched out on the chilly steel, naked, waiting to boil the metallic smell of spiritual prophylaxis, woggy amphetamine, ubiquitous compromise, and London itself off his virginal body. He waited in his stainless tub for the woman to turn the big red wheel and send him a rush of what he half trusted would be hot mineral water. But it turned out to be warmed-over tap drippings. Rusty, but potable, of course. (If you want to see if a Brit has all his teeth, just ask him if it's okay to drink the water in his country.)

Then, instead of more clever things, Sam's brain heard a voice wafting across the Atlantic and into his ears, from the pickled wastes of the Mormons' Promised Land—second driest state in the union, absorbing less than thirteen inches per year of measurable precipitation, moister only than Nevada, causing an understandable obsession with all manner of baths among its cleanly natives, including blood baths.

Hear you now the words of the Prophet Father Brigham Young, regarding the Doctrine of Blood Atonement, as held by the Moronic Myrmidons of Moloch:

"There are sins that men commit for which they simply cannot receive forgiveness in this world, nor in that which is to come; and if they had their eyes open to see their true condition, they would be willing to have their blood spilt on the dry ground, that the smoke thereof might ascend to Heaven as an offering for their sins; and the smoking incense, the fragrant steam that rises off newly shed blood, would atone for their sins. Whereas, if such is not the case, they will stick to them—"

(*They* being the sins and *them* being the sinners. Watch your referents, Brother Brig, you semi-literate, bloodthirsty motherfucker.)

"—and remain upon them in the spirit world—"

(Notice how this guy lets slip the phrase *spirit world*? Hear the blatant paganism? Why not the Bosom of Abraham? Or Beulah's Mighty Threshold?)

"—and I know that when you hear my brethren telling about cutting people off from the earth, you may consider it strong doctrine—"

(Strong medicine, ugh—you've been spending too much time with the little Navaho boys, Bro.)

"—but it is to save them, not to destroy them.

"Oh, and, by the way, fellas," continues Big 'n Hung, "now if you huff and puff and you finally save enough money for to take your wife and kids on a trip across the sea, take a tip before you take a trip a-lemme tell ya where t' go. Go to Engl-and, ohhhh..."

> *Engl-and shwangs like a pendulum do:*
> *Elders on bicycles two-by-two,*
> *The Doctrine and the Cov'nants*
> *And the Pearl o' Great Price*
> *Tell us guzzlin' London tea-hee*
> *Is a terri-bibble vice...*

> *Engl-and shwangs like a pendulum do:*
> *Elders on bicycles two-by-two.*
> *Johnny Donne's pulpit,*
> *Belial's doctrine.*
> *And it's time to take your leave*
> *Before your prick goes limp again.*

Sam sent his own voice echoing over the waves to Brother Brigham's grave in the upper avenues of Salt Lake City, or across the ether to his seraglio on his personal planet, or wherever the fuck this particular patriarch was hanging out these days.

"My eyes are open to my true condition, Brig, and it stinks so bad that neither the spilt blood nor the smoking incense thereof will sweeten this little hand."

Before he left the bathing booth, Sam reached down, gathered up his fatty soap, and created something written on the tiny rust- and pus-flecked mirror. Mixing his cursive with his printed, his upper case with his lower, in the quirky penmanship that a certain alienist had long before told his mom was a crying warning of early personality disintegration, Sam wrote—

Me*L*chi*Z*ed*Æ*k
r*U*Le,
*o*K.

Then he got himself, minus abandoned fabulous banjo, back underground quickly, like a mushroom, before his swollen pores could suck in an acid rainy chill. He placed himself on a train full of bodies with fascist newspapers instead of heads, and he thrashed, screamed and flashed through the mud tunnels, back under the silver Thames.

* * * *

At St. Pancras Station, waiting for the train to Heathrow, Sam happened to see the old English gentleman, and recognized him in a flash: the first Londoner he'd laid eyes on as his train had pulled in so long ago. Incredible coincidence, in this city of so many millions of souls, that this old English gentleman should also be the last.

It was the exact dark-blue three-piece suit, with the same misplaced elephant labia growing in vertical rolls on either side of the identical groin area, and the precise eyeballs, grey and amazed, bugged a full span as by sheer hydraulic hypertension from the hair-free Churchillian skull.

And Sam's burnt eyes simply could not read the flapping letters and numbers on the elevated schedule board, so he decided to approach this older, but kindred spirit from this other dying, whimpering nation, also older.

Sam abandoned British restraint, which he'd never mastered, anyway, and he temporarily forgot about his delayed-reaction rage, vaguely protracted, built up over the sunless, damp, grey months until it was like a computer program that could run itself; and he began to murmur, then babble, then shout in the face of the old English gentleman, right there in the concrete middle of St. Pancras Station. Literally thousands of the Queen's subjects were definitely not listening or staring.

"Might you be familiar, Sir, with the medical term keratonitis? It designates a cornea that puckers gradually from birth into the shape of a dunce cap. This is a condition associated anecdotally with congenital facial deformities. I will be blind, they say, Sir, in five years. I should not be here, and wouldn't be, if not for the efforts of a certain person. And you know as well as I, Sir, the identity of the instigator of the foul alliance that put her away for good. And there are certain misdeeds so heinous—wouldn't you agree, Sir?—that neither penance nor the love of Jesus Christ Himself will ever wash them away, but only the blood of the perpetrator himself, Sir, and—"

The old English gentleman interrupted. He raised a pale hand, more than two fingers extended. He glared icily, and, with indignation in his voice, puffed, "I don't know you. I don't care to know anyone resembling you. You look and sound half-dead, and your clothing is lamentable. I wish you would go away now."

Why I Never Walk Through a Chinese Park During Spring Festival

In China, it's impossible to become a man.
Lu Xun

The civic authorities have drained the artificial lake, and thousands of handcarts are purging the bed of five centuries' accumulation of mucus, slopping it everywhere ankle-deep. They are late for Spring Festival for the first time in a few thousand years of recorded history, demonstrating the relative merits of emperors and politburos.

This being the post-Liberation period, everybody in the city has to take a turn manning a shovel, unless he or she can afford, with discretion, to hire and exploit a substitute. Abusing my exalted position as a "foreign expert", I terrorized one of my tubercular grad students into taking my place; but, even so, I wear high-topped, laced-up Red Wing boots, after the manner of first-world proles.

I'm afraid of accidentally dragging even one booted toe in the residue that covers the street. According to my physician back home, who admittedly diagnosed himself with hypercautionary Sinophobia, the mud throughout communist-held territory in Asia is infested with hideous snails that are, in turn, infested with microscopic wormlets that burrow into the pads of your feet and slither up through your legs and pelvis, up, up, till they get to your liver and turn it to smelly gristle.

I've been invited to banquets with important provincial cadres where trenchers full of such gastropods were brought out, and I've grabbed chopsticks out of Long Marchers' hands, screaming, "Wait a second! You're not even supposed to step on those little cock-suckers!" But almost nobody heeded my warning, and nobody died. So I assume it's a matter of building up immunities over the millennia.

Spread nastily before me today in the middle of the park is a mythical quagmire. Mushed deep inside, under the more recent top layer of discarded scum-bags (three sizes, one color), verminous creatures guard a treasure. There are stories around town of snail-resistant people finding ancient perforated coins and jade bracelets. Someone was shot for trying to smuggle out a rotten skull with ruby-inlaid porcelain teeth. The periphery is crawling with Peoples' Liberation Army men.

Beyond that periphery, just out of those PLA men's eyeshot,

tucked behind South China foliage in a quadrant of jungle where, incredibly, humanity's pullulation thins out for a brief space, a certain former Red Guard used to camp out. He still squats there among the shadows, for all I know, foursquare in his formidable integrity. We don't exactly keep in touch. I was a friend of his family, in a manner of speaking, and I admired him, but he never returned the compliment.

His name was Bu Yu, and he resented my large alien presence in the Flowery Middle Kingdom. He took it into his head to re-start the Great Proletarian Cultural Revolution, at least to the limited extent necessary to dislodge me, one way or another. His objective was to deliver the local university students, merchants, civil servants and party apparatchiks out from under my Red Wing boot, which he, perhaps not altogether unfairly, considered to be planted square in the middle of everyone's faces.

To suggest that Bu Yu was mentally unbalanced would be less than sporting; but it's fair to say that he didn't have his mental finger set firmly on the political pulse of his fellow townsmen. They were just as delighted as any other southern Chinamen when Deng Xiaoping gave them permission to get back in touch with those petty entrepreneurial instincts which had, since time immemorial, defined their tribe. It would have been easier for Bu Yu to foment socialist rebellion in Beverly Hills. The snack hawkers in particular loved having me stalk their sidewalks, a ringer for Santa Claus, the very embodiment of acquisitiveness and bourgeois self-indulgence.

Bu Yu had recoiled from the sight of me, and had gone into self-imposed exile at a street boys' secret forest-encampment, located on the bank of the stream that fed the periodically drained lake. He spent his nights sleeping like a Mongolian on clay, surrounded by yellow industrial suds that caked up on the riverbank, and he passed his days growing a beard that was supposed to convince the more superstitious street boys that he was an ancient and wise man.

I do, however, know of at least one youngster, a bright daisy-colored comrade, who saw in the beard nothing more than facial hair--sparse at that, particularly compared to the dazzling array of stawberry-blond nipple-ticklers that hung off the jutting jaw of his role-model, hero, and god on earth--namely, me. I suborned the little sycophant to serve as my eyes and ears on the riverbank, and fetch me weekly reports on the babblings of Bu Yu, my mortal adversary--and my own hero, in many ways. I hope that doesn't sound too other-embracingly white and liberal. Or maybe masochistic.

Once in a while indigenous water people appeared before Bu Yu's eyes, floating among crackling bubbles on their tiny bamboo houseboats as they'd done since prehistoric times, the only members of the non-criminal classes in China who'd been assigned to no particular work unit. They wore a new expression on their faces for the first time in twenty thousand years: one of bewilderment over the increasing skimpiness and somatic strangeness of the fish they caught.

"Do we eat this extra fin or worship it?" they seemed to ask each other in the unwritten language that nobody but the few dwindling dozen of them understood. For all his political theory, Bu Yu was unable to offer advice, and so would remain speechless till they drifted out of sight.

When dirty magazines from Hong Kong appeared for the first time under the pile of banana leaves that constituted the boys' secret assembly hall, Bu Yu had waded out to purge them, to fling them far across the face of the waters. The froth had stung his feet, tough as they'd become on his shoeless meanderings during the Ten Years' Chaos. He decided at that moment to sleep henceforth with his lower extremities immersed, the pain seeping up and up into his brain and increasing the ardor of the bad-element anarchist who'd been usurping control of his dreams ever since the "opening of the doors" to outlanders like me.

Finally a kind of emery paper formed on his soles and insteps, a reptile skin composed ambiguously of Bu Yu himself and some foreign material. He became wedded to a sensation such as I imagine the desert peoples of Wulumuqi felt in their purification rites, back in the days before the light of Marxist-Leninist-Mao Zedong Thought was brought to bear on their backward mentalities. They performed week-long geothermal ablutions to undermine the structural integrity of the epidermis, then coated themselves with a pepper sauce, not unlike the stuff rich Sichuanese put in their capitalist-class food by way of condiment. But the Wulumuqi sauce was poison outright, a body lotion that reamed out the skin pores and induced pathological ecstasy.

Occasionally he even used the suds in the mornings to wash those few parts of his face unobscured by hair. Bu Yu flung himself on his belly in the glutinous sand and submerged that part of him which takes the place of a conscience in the Oriental constitution. It was a display of raw fearlessness calculated to impress children, whose nerve endings remain so much more tenderly attached than our own. And it inspired even higher levels of astonishment than he'd expected.

Perhaps the sallow spume took some visual effect upon Bu Yu's flesh that was awesome. He had no way of ascertaining for sure, as mirrors were never brought to the no-girls-allowed encampment, and the river was too adulterated with opaque substances to be reflective, even at its frequent sluggish moments. Nevertheless, if witnessing Bu Yu perform his morning toilet inspired the majority of his followers to respect and fear him more, my own precocious spy was merely put off by what I'd tutored him to regard as demagogic exhibitionism. I made sure there was always at least one sour puss in the bunch.

Having failed to muster his former comrades-in-arms (they'd all sunk into premature middle age and become beauticians or career TV-university students), Bu Yu was forced to lower his sights. He was surrounded by a kindergarten full of children instead of an army of seasoned Red Guards who struggled, and maimed while struggling. The excessive zealot, the tooth-gritting, gore-gushing fanatic soldier of a decade ago, had been reincarnated on the riverbank as a whacker of flowers with thorn switches, a marksman with rubber band-powered, pebble-loaded slingshots: not a rebellion-maker, but an aimless vandal, a future candidate for the triad gangs if somebody didn't take him in hand.

But Bu Yu sensed that maturity didn't matter at this point, if the boys could be directed firmly away from their inherited bad-element leanings and toward political consciousness in his newly instituted Hong Xiaoxue program, his outdoor Red Elementary School.

He had tried at first, through incentives such as free fish-fries, to up the membership, to "cook" as many lads as possible and cement their loyalty. In a momentary confusion brought on by dismay over the moral decay of this town's latest generation, he'd lost sight of the original plan and become convinced that his presence on the river could be justified only by large numbers of converts. As though he were some Jesus-possessed missionary, Bu Yu had wanted to redeem children like pawned possessions, revealing more about his own upbringing than I'm sure he would have liked.

But soon enough he returned to his senses, and was even forced to take contrary measures to limit membership. For, like all well-planned organizations, this one had to be arranged along auspicious numerological lines. The inner circle could number neither more nor less than thirty-five, seven times five, threescore and ten divided by two, which happened to be the exact age of both Bu Yu and the adversary, who lived in somewhat plusher quarters among actual grown-ups in town.

That would be me, of course, but Bu Yu had chosen not to specify as much, just yet, at least not in the ears of the more babyish infantrymen, for fear of frightening them off altogether. Though a sweet man, and ludicrously out of shape--a jolly old elf, in fact--I am half again as tall, and three times as heavy, as the average Chi-com, with devil-colored eyes that seem especially to trouble children on the street when I'm in a certain mood. Bu Yu was right to be reluctant to introduce my specifications into the camp dialectic. But my spy made sure that plenty of unauthorized scuttlebutt regarding "the adversary's" identity seeped down into the awareness of the lowliest grunts in the trenches, causing a good number of them to go AWOL.

Eventually Bu Yu would be obliged to begin setting up the infrastructure of offices and commands that would provide a solid backbone for his miniature army. Once the members had mellowed a bit and the real business of class struggle could commence, there'd need to be a secretariat, along with teams in charge of materials and propaganda, liaison and external affairs, finance and logistics, plus a special task force for armed combat and its preparations.

All this would be based on fond memories of the brave rebellion-making force he'd belonged to during the best years of his life. I sometimes wonder, looking back, if it was symptomatic of encroaching age when this commie hero of mine spent a greater amount of his free time imagining bureaucratic maneuvers than planning specific skirmishes to come.

Before Bu Yu could bore these congenital anarchists with the dry realities of organized class war, he had to make the encampment seem like an esoteric fraternity, to appeal to their primitive instincts. He remembered the entertaining lies about old gangster societies that the peasants had poured into his own preadolescent ears during the forced rustications, and he applied them here at the twig and tendril fort: the freemasonry borrowed from protestant missionaries; the qi gong spells and formulaic gyrations; the time-telling from observing the dilations of cats' eyes--all the rudimentary psychological and physiological magic that would soon lead up to the more correct Red Book-wielding loyalty dances.

At the same time he tried to avoid corrupting these green brains with the more metaphysical superstitions which he and his middle-school classmates had combatted so hard in the short-lived

Four Olds Movement. Those belief systems slithered out of one's guts, up and up, transgressed beyond simple magic, and approached the insidious pathology called religion. But he had a suspicion that his scrupulosity was wasted on many of the thinner, more raggedy recruits, who'd been saturated already with such poison by their toothless grannies at bedtime, judging from the Daoistic way they scampered home as soon as the sun began to sink and the river turned blood-red.

Whenever the mauled carcass of a large fanged monkey washed downstream from the mountaintops, Bu Yu had to shout reality back into their ears before they could bolt: "Of course wild pigs are strong enough to rip their heads in half like that!" Then, allowing the dialectical materialist in him to get the better of the youth recruiter, he would incautiously add a rhetorical question: "What other creature up there could do it?"

The children had a whole bestiary of other creatures, most possessing three or four eyes and combustible breath, or, more terrifying still, two eyes, two legs, language and self-consciousness.

It was exactly their fear of violent death that made the substance of blood wield power over their small imaginations. So Bu Yu had risked later revolutionary historians' accusing him of feudalistic tendencies, and had introduced blood oaths of secrecy into the riverside ceremonial. This flattered his followers into believing that he valued their confidence and that he assumed somebody in their lives, a teacher, parent, or even a neighborhood committeewoman, would care enough to listen if they revealed their new uncle's unregistered presence outside the city walls.

The blood was derived from depriving oneself of the first layer of skin on the barest tip of the fifth finger of the right hand, or the left, whichever seemed more profound and symbolical to the particular bleeder, instead of removing the whole first joint, which had been the method of dynastic bandits. A generation of sons returning home each night lacking body parts might call attention to their enclave.

As for me, I wouldn't be willing to bet foreign exchange currency that such dismemberment would cause much of a stir in the degenerate small-time hawker households many of the more unfortunate little soldiers came from. It was, after all, a city of shopkeepers. Confronted with surgical stitches across their offspring's torso, these fine burghers would just ask for a percentage of the price the missing organs had fetched on the overseas black market.

Even the less deprived boys tended to be elementary school dropouts, alienated already from their papas, those traitors to the cause of socialism, outright royalists and opportunistic glommers-on to the line of the old saboteur Deng Xiaoping. It was small cause to wonder that such fathers had failed to maintain even twelve years' worth of filial piety from their sons, and no surprise that such sons should have established a secret family of their own, with a home base made of sticks and straw that doubled as a mock fortification in their daddy-annihilating army games.

At least it would not be necessary to drive one traditional weakness from the hearts of the Hong Xiaoxue enrollees. None of them could be said to suffer from feudal familism, the central flaw that had held China back from achieving true proletarian dictatorship all these millennia. Bu Yu himself had set a fine example by breaking with his own clan, effecting a final and cleanly split--except for one sweet, lovely pink propinquity that nobody (least of all I) could blame him for clinging to, in his private heart.

* * * *

The charter members had stumbled onto this more or less secluded spot by deciphering fifteen-year-old inscriptions scratched on rocks and banyan trees by their uncles, the local Red Guards, on their junior long marches and on-foot linkups. Upon hearing that Bu Yu had been around during that remote and legendary antiquity, the boys had agreed by informal consensus to put him up, a black-skinned jester for their kingless court.

But, ever so gradually, he could sense it now, they were developing an interest not only in his eccentricities of speech and personal hygiene, but also in what he had to say about the great world beyond the ferns and fronds that shaded them here. Bu Yu was able to recapture a portion of his former rhetorical fervor, and his Hong Xiaoxue was beginning to take shape, as were the embryonic political consciousnesses of the lads. The family was developing a proper daddy.

He knew full well that encouraging children to stay away from their mothers' breakfasts and their schools' lunches was illegal. But Liu Shao Qi's organizing the An Yuan miners in 1927 was also illegal, in the extreme, and he was expelled from the politburo as a rightist. That did not hinder him, and the result was the glorious Autumn Harvest Uprising--an inspirational story Bu Yu was saving to tell the children after he'd laid a bit more theoretical groundwork in their heads.

At the school sessions disguised as impoverished fish-fries, he began his first formal attempts to instruct his charges in the principles of Red combat maneuverability and the Lo Ming line of guerilla tactics. This was seen by them as absurd at first, ensconced as they were in a leafy lean-to fortress they deemed impregnable by natural means.

"It's impregnable only in the sense that your sole enemies at this point are your fat-assed fathers who are too lazy and too bourgeois to muddy their feet by following you out here and dragging you back home to your school books."

"But, Teacher," said one of the few cooperative students (my personal mole-boy, in fact, who'd been instructed to feed lines to the commandant, and memorize any responses), "why do our fathers refuse to muddy their feet? For fear of the liver worms?"

"The what? No. Of course not. It's because muddy feet will make them look like peasants, and they would rather lose their sons than slip down a single notch on their topsy-turvy scale of class stratifications. Their social-climbing affectations deprive them of heirs, and yet they believe that those latch-keys strung about your necks will somehow prevent your love from drying up like a pig turd on a suburban sidewalk."

Very few of them had been listening, but several ears perked up at the mention of pig turds. Bu Yu had to remind himself not to allow the juvenile's traditional love of pig turd jokes to adulterate his style of public speaking on a permanent basis; for someday he hoped to address grown-ups again.

He continued.

"But when there is a real enemy to be struggled, and when that enemy is fatter and taller and nastier than you, and his arrogance is only exceeded by his contemptuous lack of concern for you, then you must leave your little fort and go to him rather than wait for his siege engines to pull up to the gate. Then the Lo Ming line of guerilla tactics is the best method not only of survival but of prevailing. Chairman Mao exhorts us never to fight an unprepared war. Allow me to demonstrate."

And he would squat and draw, in the greasy sediment underfoot, battle schematics from recent and remote revolutionary history, while the boys who were interested gathered around, some without thought resting little hands on his shoulders.

"You Hong Xiaoxue tongshimen are looking for a road and a line to take," he said in a more tender voice, "though many of you don't even know it now. I will provide you with a road and a line, and an enemy to annihilate."

One effeminate tag-along child, from a family of low-level municipal clerks, thoroughly out of place, was just unvigorous enough to have sat still and listened to Bu Yu's hints, and just bright enough to have divined that there was a specific personage against whom they were to mobilize. He raised his reedy voice high enough to be heard over the general babble, and pleaded lenience, incredibly enough, on behalf of this as-yet-officially-unspecified enemy.

"But, Teacher, he has a wife. And a child, too. At least I've seen him spending a lot of time with a young girl in the park. Is it dialectical materialism to interfere with someone's papa?"

After a gasp and a terrifying dive deep into his own infantile memory (a certain female face leered up at him from the murk), Bu Yu's innermost guts recognized this sissy-boy's strange sense of anonymous mercy, as sure as if it had been his own weakness in a previous incarnation.

Mercy was the womanish characteristic that would one day make life on earth surpass the sweetest feudal fantasy of Heaven. But not until the revolution was complete and true proletarian dictatorship had been achieved all over the world. And, until that remote moment, this compassion, so generalized, so indiscriminate and so pointless in a materialistic universe, would be nothing less than a purulent ulcer on the side of his rebellion-making youth corps. Bu Yu must suture this wound shut before any ideological pus could slosh into the other boys' brains.

"You, child," he hissed, "are adopting the Chen Tu-Hsiu line of right-opportunist reconciliationism that brought catastrophe to our party in the spring of 1928."

The words were unimportant at this point. But Bu Yu's voice and face were filled with jeering contempt which caused the simpler individuals to laugh and ridicule the weakling among them. Their scorn was free of the murderous indignation that must come in later purges, but it served its purpose. The runt ran home sobbing through suds and mud, into the arms of his no doubt love-bloated Christian-convert maternal relative.

The worst kind. The kind you love and admire. That brings death. The best are those toward whom you can feel a tender condescension as they fetch you bowls of rice. But it were better to have one who physically tortured you, taught you early the meaning of the dislocated joint, the twisted bowel, the spoon-gouged eye, than gorged you on the syrup of her mammalian love. How well Bu Yu knew this.

I knew it too, from introducing myself to his family (loving females included) in the city park before the snail cataclysm. And he was right to have split from them: the Bu family was a bunch of grinning, feeble saps, standard self-loathing third-world types. They were giddy at the honor of a big Caucasoid condescending to be a "friend of the family" (so to speak), yet ashamed and apologetic about a certain camped-out relative of theirs--a stalwart who, in spite of his murderous feelings toward me, I wouldn't have hesitated to claim, in a loud voice, as my own twin brother.

I had even fewer compunctions about claiming his little sister as one of my own. She was Bu Yu's tender pride and hopeful joy, the compact personification of everything pure and dialectically materialistic in his heart's deep scarlet chambers. This was, after all, the People's Republic, with an emphasis on the possessive, and female comrades were to be valued as nowhere else in all of the extreme orient.

With Big Brother gone among the revolutionists, the child needed firm male guidance, which I felt it my duty to provide, as I was the cause of the fraternal vacancy in her darling existence. Nearly twenty years younger than us both, making her jailbait outright in any civilized country, she was the most lascivious little trough of slop I'll ever make a swine of myself over. My Red Wing may have been planted on everyone else's face during the day, but I shrink from telling you what sweet red thing was planted on mine in the early evenings--at least until mud-snails rendered our special cranny in the park inaccessible. (That Big Brother was not supposed to know should be obvious, but I emphasized it with warmth to my spy, anyway.)

Hence the merciful Christian-convert boy's innocent misapprehension that I was "someone's papa." From the moment he fled in the face of Bu Yu's sarcasm until he came back pleading for readmission, kowtowing his forehead audibly on the riverbank, this weeping weenie was tailed by his coevals on the streets as a security risk. But readmitted he was, for he would have constituted something of a loss. At least he was useful as an attention-getter. When not expelling or re-embracing him, the recruits were interested only in talking about food.

Bu Yu had so far been unable to provide them with much to eat besides deformed river vermin. He'd taught them a few of the old partisan tricks, like luring out, capturing and consuming live the frogs from under rocks in stagnant pools. While not exactly tasty or filling, they were supposed to make you clever, devious and slippery as an amphibian, just as gouts of sap made you tall as the tree they oozed from. These qualities presumably compensated for the strength you lacked from chewing on frogs and sap instead of the fat sides of town pigs. And, on market days, it was possible to glean a few vitamins from vegetable garbage floating by--but sand-scrub the diesel off or die.

As for the youngsters who, thanks to their innately superior class consciousness, or maybe just abusive parents, had already come under his sway and cooperativized themselves permanently at his side on the riverbank, Bu Yu could only try to supplement their diets with pilfered rice hay from the hillside paddy terraces, made more substantial with a healthy smearing of mineral-rich jungle clay.

There was the festival that had survived the Four Olds Movement, where the tea farmers upstream threw zongzi of glutinous rice and sweet red beans into the water, ghost confections which Commander Bu Yu retrieved and rationed for weeks afterward. He tried to convince the ungrateful boys that the farmers were not to be considered especially backward just because they didn't gobble these rice cakes themselves, as had become the custom in recent centuries among townsmen who'd finally learned to scoff correctly at spirits.

"Superstitious, yes. But there is a certain progressiveness about the farmers' admiration of the poet/hero whose waterlogged spirit those zongzi are intended to placate. He was a true proto-revolutionary who scorned the advances of the emperor, though his writings are not entirely free from reactionary characteristics."

But this politicization of the semi-dissolved rice cakes failed to get their minds off food. In those increasingly rare times when Bu Yu could get them to talk about the objective of their struggle, even that got twisted in a culinary direction.

One boy stood and said, "I've heard that when a Chinese gets no vegetables or fruit for ten years, his hair will turn the foreigners' color, the color of northern Shaanxi pine tree ears, or a fine Mandarin orange after you've peeled it, and you're about to take a bite." (A flattering image for my ginger mop; but I'll take it.)

"You don't mean it!" snarled the most theatrically inclined of them all, a big-eyed and -eared boy who'd been designated this tribe's

Master of the Games before Bu Yu's sport-spoiling arrival. "You don't mean the very same color of the beard that hangs from the jaw of the baby-eating devil, Doctor San Mu Ai De Wen?"

"Oh, no! Hide!"

The usual Nanjing-style soldier's riot followed hard on the mention of that weird name. Bu Yu's living forces reverted to the savage condition to which they, in their extreme youth, lived in such close proximity. They commenced indulging in a strange apotropaic ritual, a primitive monster game or drama with assigned roles and memorized lines, featuring a bad spirit that Bu Yu did not recall from his own brainless baby years--but then, he'd been raised in a more enlightened time, the Great Leap Forward, when such feudal shades had been briefly banished from the land.

"I'm Doctor San Mu Ai De Wen!" screamed one boy, looming large while the others feigned terror. "That means I have three mothers, and I help spread the plague wherever I go! I'm going to tear the front of your father's house down!"

"It's Three-Mothers-Aids-the-Plague! Hide!"

The sillier and younger ones squealed like girls and ran to conceal their minuscule maidenheads in the bushes, so as not to be caught and eaten by a figment of their collective imagination that resembled me.

Back in town, their commandant had recoiled from my physical presence too quickly to have memorized enough of my external characteristics to make the connection himself. And, for all his talk of "propaganda" and "liaison" and "external affairs" and "logistics," Bu Yu had never mastered my name, barbarian monikers being the wrong shape to sit comfortably in any but the most youthful and flexible Chinese mind. That's why the boys had so charmingly transliterated "Dr. Samuel Edwine" into their gutter idiom, together with that wry literal rendering of the Sinicized syllables.

Bu Yu's brain, which, like mine, had been calcified to the normal extent after languishing half a lifetime on this earth, remained mystified as to the who-and-what of this lecture-disrupting bugbear, this contagious San Mu-Whatever, who, unique among dynastic demons, possessed not only a trio of loving moms, but a doctorate (mail-ordered from the back pages of Hustler, by the way). My spy was not about to enlighten him.

The boys who were hiding from me in the bushes forgot their hunger only until bulbs of vegetable matter depending from various twigs reminded them again.

"If that's the color of the Doctor's hair," said someone, who remained in the character of a cowering little girl and dreamily licked a lascivious red blossom, "does it mean that all barbarian intelligentsia don't get enough vitamins?"

"Of course they do. Foreigners eat more than two jin of meat for lunch."

"And jiaozi dumplings, two jin, for their supper."

Bu Yu decided to let this conversation run its course. If the troops would rather discuss victuals than ideology, so be it. Correctness grows directly from the judicious satisfaction of such needs. They had to be fed, he knew. But not as much as adolescents or full-grown men.

And there was another advantage, among the countless disadvantages, of working with children. While wringing one's hands over their diet, at least one didn't need to worry about procuring camp followers for them as well. They were too young to know, first of all, that they needed copulation, and, second, that they didn't need it at all.

Sitting and staring at all these sets of ribs, naked and horizontal under the shimmering trees, Bu Yu was reminded in a terrible way of the Venetian blinds, western-style Hong Kong imports, that he'd once ripped from a certain high provincial cadre's office in late 1964. "Other comrades work by sunlight and burn themselves black to feed the revolution," young Bu Yu had sneered, "while you prefer the twilight of the feudal opium den!"

"What have you to hide, Bad Element Lao Ren?" the Red Guards had screamed at the old man in the glorious struggle session later that afternoon, when blood vessels exploded in his wife's saggy temples and reduced her to a lopsided, drooling burden that had to be shot for her own good, as soon as they were able to liberate a working AK-47 from the army.

In those days the busy youth of China had to be reminded, even persuaded, to swallow a few grains of rice once in a while. But now hear their successors whine.

The next boy to speak was the son of a black-class merchant. He declaimed an invisible inventory across the face of the ruined river.

"Foreigners have the biggest blood peaches, and all the immortality noodles they can swallow, plus safety eggs, boiled just right, not too tough, even when it's not their birthday."

Feeling like a joyless schoolmarm tromping on a forty-points game with both big feet, just to join in on the fun (for there were fun moments when he was young, weren't there?), Bu Yu decided to step in and provide some cultural background that he hoped was innocuous and not too feudal. Perhaps, directed toward the allegorical, the boys could be gradually steered away from the gastronomical and toward the political.

"Yes," he grinned, "and do you comrades know why our ancient great-great-great grannies from time gone by called them immortality noodles? It's because noodles are long and thin, like the number one, and safety eggs are round, like the number zero, and together they make one hundred, the best age we could wish to attain on our birthdays, and--"

Someone scoffed loudly at this point. It was a brazen boy (guess who), older than the others, almost a youth, on the borderline of not belonging here. He was strong and, I'm pleased to affirm, well-fed: clearly it wasn't necessity but curiosity which brought him to the encampment (or maybe he was just running an errand for someone large and pale and evil, a great blond beast who lurked nearby). In one of the more recent mumbo-jumbo ceremonies, Bu Yu, smelling this kid's talent, but not his treachery, had hastily pronounced him Commissar, hoping to co-opt his aggressiveness with the flattery of a title.

This commissar had received a superior education by local standards, reactionary though it was, at the local key school, where he'd actually paid attention. He was aware, and tried to impress upon the few kiddies who might be persuaded to care, that their self-proclaimed commander had virtually no formal schooling, like most of his generation, who'd made rebellion, not term papers.

Our bright commissar now announced to the others that Bu Yu's immortality noodle "nonsense" was a pathetic example of the midget sense of history the Red Guards had developed between rampages during the Ten Years' Chaos. And no wonder "Mao's little generals" were so easily duped into throwing themselves into a short-lived movement that all of China had rejected in hindsight.

Bu Yu almost howled with horror and indignation.

The commissar ignored him and continued. "We only began to use western digits like one and zero after Liberation. And birthdays are recent also, at least among mainstream Han Chinese. What's your ethnicity, Commander? Up until the very late Qing Dynasty most people simply added to their ages every New Years' Day. How 'ancient,' then, can your stupid immortality noodle tradition be, Commander? Besides, I thought immortality was a feudal superstition, and that when we die our bodies turn into minerals useful for production and so on."

In the stunned hush that followed such a cheeky utterance, someone started a rumor which was to remain in brisk circulation long after this Hong Xiaoxue was disbanded, each twig and tendril of its fortifications washed downstream to clog the artificial lake: the commissar was believed to be a thirty-year-old genius dwarf party member, a trained expert ideological saboteur planted in the ranks by the very high provincial cadre whose wife and Venetian blinds Bu Yu had destroyed back in '64. And that wasn't too wide of the mark. He was indeed planted, but not by any old Chinaman. He was my protege, my handiwork--also younger sibling, coincidentally, to the tubercular grad student who was obliging enough to be scooping a certain foreigner's quota of lake mucus at that very moment.

It was high time for this small cooperative's second political purge. Bu Yu would try to nail my boy on class composition: his father was no doubt intelligentsia with foreign leanings, his mother a black class cur, his older brother a craven mud-scraping toady to the enemy.

But in the meantime it was essential to remain as calm as possible in front of one's inferiors. Bu Yu maintained his dignity--or that part of it which hadn't just been sand-blasted away. He considered not even making an immediate reply. But to say nothing at all would be to lose even more face. So he took a breath and murmured something like, "From what Guomindang rightist pamphlet, smuggled by which fishing boat, across which quadrant of the Taiwan Straits, did you, with your typical petite-bourgeois schoolboy's memory, plagiarize that, Comrade Commissar?"

"Huh?" said more than one of the others.

Bu Yu lost no time in labeling my mole a putschist. He forced him to undergo thought-remolding in the deep jungle alongside another boy, also a putschist. Bu Yu deliberately lumped together the two most dissimilar, yet most dangerous individuals. This would serve to confuse and distract the others from the counterrevolutionary content of their respective lines.

The other putschist liked to be called The Horseman, in honor of his favorite group activity: circle-jerking (which, like scissors-paper-rock and so many other cultural advances, originated in China). "Riding the Horse" signifies jacking off in gutter Mandarin; and, in this sense, The Horseman played Master Bates to the commissar's Artful Dodger. He even had the irritatingly ready laugh that characterizes his guild of specialists.

He was a Li Lisan-type neo-Bolshevik adventurist who wanted to kidnap my wife and send bits of her body in the mail to various places. He didn't care where, and wasn't worried about the postage. He considered that part a mere detail, a concern of the pencil pushers in the liaison office that Bu Yu had yet to establish.

This sordid self-abusing creature happened to have a little sister of his own, just like Bu Yu, and he had once offered to bring her to the encampment for everybody to "enter her meat" (literal translation), including Bu Yu, if "the commander used only the back garden and some soybean oil," which he offered to furnish in a plastic bag for a small extra charge.

In trying to get his fellows to give him a few fen in advance, The Horseman explained, "My father has intended to turn her out since she was born. From the time she could walk till now, ten years later, he has never allowed Little Sister to wear any clothes on the lower half of her body when she plays in the streets, not even in winter. And she must relieve herself openly on the sidewalk, like a baby, so she will grow accustomed to thinking of herself as public property. Socialistic, eh?"

When Bu Yu reacted with violent revulsion, the faceless rodent shrugged and said, "It beats slashing her throat at birth, which is what my uncles do to daughters. She has no civil existence, anyway, because she was born in violation of the one-child policy."

This little monster had once flung a stone and brained a Honda-riding boar hunter from a fire-watch brigade situated in the hills above them, and had stolen, or "requisitioned," as he put it, an extremely rare thing these days: a privately owned rifle. It was an ancient wide-bore dynastic make, a regular artifact, weighing at least twenty jin. The one time it was fired the roar was loud enough to produce waves on the surface of the river and bring shapeless, pale things up from the bottom. The Horseman had vowed to climb up on a park bench and discharge his artillery straight into one of my eye sockets. Fortunately he was not finding it easy, even with his sister's intercession, to procure more ammunition.

"That's all right," he leered, exposing his chafed self. "I'll just shoot my spare cannon in the strugglee's eye instead."

Elder sibling, himself, to a sweet pepper sprout of girl who had just managed to squeeze into existence under the one-child wire, Bu Yu found it difficult not to purge this evil brat on the spot, using a big rock. But he restrained himself. The Horseman was the ideal sort of maniac to class with the dangerous commissar, in order to discredit the latter in the eyes of the few circumspect youngsters.

Bu Yu might chain the commissar to such filth for thought-remolding, but rejected the idea of purging my boy completely. He was, after all, one of the few campers aware of something besides his own digestive tract. He had imagination, I'm proud to say, and even rudimentary socialist sensibilities--at least to the extent that I was able to coach him on such cobwebby relics of outmoded historico-political woolgathering.

For example, he'd been the only one not to scoff at Bu Yu's suggestion that they recruit some actual peasant-class boys into their small cooperative, some tea farmers' sons perhaps, in order to combat Stalinist/Comintern urban elitism among the ranks. And the commissar was willing, in spite of his professed contempt for Bu Yu, to bring useful bits of information from town, such as news about the ill-advised and naive student democracy demonstrations and their fascinating effect on the local power structure. (I'm afraid, however, that any intelligence he delivered concerning me was of the disinformative sort.)

"So, let him rebut me and try to humiliate me at political study sessions," Bu Yu was overheard mumbling to himself. "Nobody ever listens anyway."

* * * *

One afternoon, as this old Red Guard surveyed the ranks, such as they were, of the first fighting force he'd been associated with since the treacherous suppression and back-to-school order of March, 1967, he felt his heart swell. Hoping his sudden access of ardor would catch their attention and maybe even hold onto it for a while, he delivered what might be called his first bona-fide Hong Xiaoxue speech. It was a short one, but otherwise almost comparable to the soul-stirrers of his youth.

"We must run the foreigner out," he said, "but in these early stages of our movement we need to use the conservative dialectical method of 'being split in two.' We mustn't make the short-sighted blunder of the Boxers before us. We have a moral responsibility to struggle the foreigner first and awaken his class consciousness so he can return to his homeland, just as the imperialist-tool American P.O.W.'s returned from the conflict in Korea, to export the world proletarian revolt. We must at least make such an attempt or risk being classified forever as mere hooligans. Always remember, comrades, you are Mao's little yellow buffaloes, opening furrows wherever you go for the seeds of his thought to take root!"

Yawns. Mumbled observations on Mao's being dead for quite a while, and not producing much thought at all these days, as far as anybody could ascertain.

Bu Yu had thrown in too many four-character words at once, too soon. He had gotten carried away into garrulousness. He tried to win them back and to redeem the speech by introducing a little material that would strike closer to home.

"You little brothers want to talk about dead figures of national veneration? Well, I happen to know that several of your mothers keep photos and paintings of the late premier Zhou Enlai in the your hovels. But did you know that, back in 1966, he took the blatantly revisionist line of protecting the big-noses on Beijing's embassy lane from the righteous wrath of the Red Guards?"

"Ho-hum. Was anybody even born yet?" jeered somebody who squatted on the rear layer of fronds--another putschist-snake wanting a purge.

The troops lost interest again. The meeting degenerated even past the point of gastronomic babble, and sank down into the childishness of sport.

Some of the older ones scattered away into the woods after crickets to pit against each other in prizefighting bouts on flattened river bed rocks. The foolhardy ones stripped and tried to submerge themselves for a swim among crispy dead fish.

Bu Yu saw that the first outright rule of comportment he'd have to enact would be a moratorium on badminton. Aside from being an effeminate game invented by British imperialists to keep their wives' lubricious thighs off the shoulders of strapping colonial serfs, the racquets and shuttlecocks themselves were distracting, a perpetual incitement to shrieking babyish chaos.

The puzzling monster game was starting up again on the quadrant of riverbank closest to his nest. The bugbear with the doctorate reappeared, who so often distracted the Hong Xiaoxue tongshimen from the real work of revolution. Bu Yu grabbed the nearest screamer and demanded to know, once and for all, who or what this Doctor San Mu Ai De Wen was supposed to be.

Before he submerged his hungry self into his role, the boy looked at Bu Yu with a fair measure of the old scorn for the blackened court jester returning to his eyes.

"How ignorant can you be at your age, Uncle? Everybody knows Three-Mothers-Aids-the-Plague. He's a giant demon, the color of Mandarin oranges after you peel them, and he'll tear the front of your father's house down and steal your baby sisters from the hammock."

"A child's imaginary villain," sniffed Bu Yu, fighting scorn with scorn. "Unreal nightmare stuff for babies only, like the adversaries of Monkey King. Not as interesting as real flesh and blood class enemies, don't you think?"

"Oh, but he is real. He spends his spare time dickering with peasants over extra girl babies for his breakfast."

"Yes," added another little comrade. "And he has a familiar fox spirit, pretty but poisonous, who rides his giant nose like a peasant straddling a water buffalo. And, in the evening, she makes scary rhythmic shrieky noises behind the bushes in the park."

They bounded off, leaving their commander with a large but blurry qualm looming in the back of his head.

* * * *

Oddly enough, it was to our commissar alone that Bu Yu wound up revealing the fullness of his intentions.

It was during one sunset, the hour when most of his living forces began to sneak off for supper with their families, leaving Bu Yu alone at the encampment with the literal waifs--little animals, uninteresting and malnourished, all staring eyes, empty bellies and emptier heads, who hung on mostly from fear of the dark.

As he made gestures toward feeding himself and them with the few mouth-stinging grey carp that floated in on the chemical foam, bloated bellies up, he tried to encourage everyone with the words his faction had always cheerfully bandied about in times of physical privation.

"This is like Soviet Russia in 1917, and look what became of them!"

The waifs were not responding. They certainly had no clue as to who or what the word "soviet" signified; and, looking into their glazed eyes, Bu Yu came to the intestine-freezing realization that they didn't even know what 1917 meant. How many is such a big number, and how many rice husks can it count into your mouth?

On this night our commissar had been assigned to stay on later than usual, ostensibly to give his commander a little companionship among these infant ghouls. With that possibility in mind, Bu Yu just started speaking in mid-thought, disburdening himself into a receptive ear for the first time since pitching camp here.

"We must make life so unpleasant for the big-nose that he leaves the Motherland and takes as many of his own kind with him as possible, and--"

Before he could take a second breath, the commissar, my ever-smooth and handy creature, interrupted Bu Yu with an almost verbatim anticipation of what he'd planned to say next. He began to express things in bright teen talk that seemed to border on something higher--but perhaps, Bu Yu, in his agitated state of mind those days, read more into the words than was really there.

Through a yawn my boy pointed out that the leave-taking itself shouldn't be too difficult to induce, as foreigners were extremely mobile and irresponsible. They had little sense of contractual honor and low tolerance for discomfort or inconvenience.

"That's exactly right," marveled Bu Yu.

After his attempts to slog into the muddled awareness of the others, Bu Yu was overwhelmed by the clarity of this youngster's brain. He deluded himself that such a brain might conceive some sympathy for him.

Trying to keep his voice from trembling with excitement, Bu Yu said, "From what I've heard, this big-nose is typical of his kind. It would mean as little to him to pack up and leave before his job is done as it apparently would to destroy the honor of one of China's pure little plum blossoms--"

Bu Yu's heart swelled at the mention of the last phrase, and he added, not thinking of the potential consequences, "Corrupting Little Sister is nothing but a five-minute's prank to this imperialist."

(I resent that--sometimes it took the better part of a quarter of an hour.)

The commissar leaned forward, eyes brightening. Bu Yu understood too late that he'd said way too much.

"And what does China's, um, little sister think of all this?" The key word was carefully enunciated to make sure this bit of intelligence had definitely passed between them.

Something inside Bu Yu, maybe simple self-loathing, now made him confess his second dirtiest secret to his second worst enemy, the one person who could do him the most damage at this point. He told our hungry-eared commissar (and therefore me) the secret he'd never considered revealing to anyone. Bu Yu had unravelled the thread of his fate to the point where beardless, ballless boys were all he had left as comrades and confessors. He hadn't intended to mention his little love; but now that he had, he couldn't prevent himself from going on. Pacing the bank, kicking the smaller urchins aside, Bu Yu pretended to be preoccupied with some serious adult matter and to be exposing his fatal secret in an offhanded manner, as though it were merely a source of minor irritation.

"As a matter of fact, I have no idea what she thinks. I haven't seen her since she was in split pants, peeing on the cobblestones. I don't want her to see what I look like now. I'm scared my whiskers will make her laugh at me in a mean way."

And that was it.

I can vouch for there being something irresistible about the amoral openness of our commissar's little face. Never mind the reason for his attentiveness: to gather ammunition to destroy Bu Yu in the only place where he'd managed to go undestroyed.

Without blinking an eye, my dwarf spy said, "Wouldn't it be my responsibility, as Commissar, to tell the others that we're mobilizing in order to resolve your personal family problem? Wasn't a war once fought in Asia Minor for such a shaky reason?"

He looked in Bu Yu's eyes and paused just long enough to extract fathomless agonies. Then he smiled and whispered, "This is a picnic for them. Why spoil it?"

Just as he was rising to go home and have supper with his family, my apt pupil turned around and, almost as an afterthought, tacked on the last of many lies he'd brought to this doomed encampment, but the first explicit untruth to exit his mouth: "I promise, on my word of socialistic honor, Commander Bu Yu, that I won't tell a soul."

* * * *

Meanwhile, downriver, at the municipal park, I'm all hunched over, trying to be debonair enough not to gag and puke at the terrible things my boots are being put through. I do my utmost to take a jaunty promenade on the elbow of the cutest and naughtiest China doll south of the Yangtze.

One slight strip of ground has been kept relatively unmuddied for the purposes of rehearsing an anemic lunar new year's celebration, or something like that. I see serried ranks of six-year-olds--those whose class consciousness Bu Yu failed to raise against me--prancing around in Year of the Rat costumes, pre-theory of subconscious-style. Glittering, scaly tails penetrate plump cheeks like child molesters' dream-penises, wiggling with coached seductiveness in time to a pirated Hong Kong disco tape.

Behind these gyrate a range of individuals gotten up to resemble an even younger brand of meat. They wear giant plastic infant heads on their shoulders. Flesh-tone body stockings make them appear bare-naked except for the traditional short aprons that keep the genders of these sham toddlers just ambiguous enough to be, one would suppose, fascinating--at least to a certain type of park-frequenting person.

Such aprons can be seen on pairs of bronze baby-statues in some of the crasser northeastern Buddhist temples. The idea is to reach under and pinch whatever slippery little lump you find. If it's a scrotum, you'll be blessed with a son. If labia--well, that unfortunate contingency can always be dealt with by other provisions in the Flowery Middle Kingdom's rich cultural heritage, usually involving a jagged implement and a patch of good earth. A shameful waste, from which my very taste buds recoil like snails from grain spirits.

The ruling party has so far failed to provide a new socialist system of esthetics to replace the more or less satisfactory pre-Liberation one they liquidated; so now the commies seem to be trying out a kind of sentimental pedophilia as part of their "bold, unprecedented modernization experiment." It's as close as their collective imagination can come to a western democratic style of public celebration. Building a culture from ashes, they expect in a few decades to cough up an emotionally nutritious set of rituals, and this is what they get: large-scale pederasty, and a painful demonstration of what Lu Xun meant when he said that it's impossible to become a man in China.

I trust Bu Yu arrived at that wisdom not long after I did.

Nite Caps

The Lord called to Samuel, who answered, "Here I am."
He ran to Eli and said, "Here I am. You called me."
"I did not call you," Eli said. "Go back to sleep."
1 Samuel 3: 4-5

During the greater part of my fourteenth year, I was obliged to pay regular visits to a certain loved one in the loony bin. I was the only person in the family who could spend any time at all in the locked ward without acting too cheerful and making everyone feel like monkeys in the zoo. In fact, I blended right in, and made several friends.

At that time a woman named Mrs Sproul was undergoing incarceration. She spent a lot of time in hydrotherapy, listening, by means of a tiny earplug, to a smuggled-in radio. She explained everything to me in no uncertain terms.

Mrs Sproul was getting extra hydrotherapy because she couldn't sleep. Almost nothing in the medicine cabinet could knock her all the way out for any curative length of time. "Maybe more baths will help," she suggested to me. "Maybe this troublesome crone will eventually resolve into a mauve sauce, and cease being able to distinguish between waking and sleeping anymore. Just sloshing."

The reason Mrs Sproul remained so wakeful was that she'd received a vague presentiment concerning the lateral motion of her son, who was a well established classical clarinetist and literary lion in London. She emphasized to me, repeatedly, that her son was no gutter minstrel. By no means did Samuel chant his tortured ditties in the tube while gnawing on an aluminum Jew's harp for shillings.

The vague presentiment--that she and Samuel would soon be sharing a continent, if they weren't doing so already--came to her late one night in conjunction with her contraband transistor radio, and ever since then she'd been listening when she got the chance, hoping to hear again whatever it was that would bring filial matters into sharper focus.

Mrs Sproul had to sneak around because this was the loony bin (to be specific, the upstairs psychiatric ward of Our Lady of Sorrows Hospital, located just kitty-corner from the Capital Casino in the incorporated municipality of Panguitch, Nevada), and you were never supposed to be exposed to the chaos outside: no phone calls or letters, not even from your family. "They could go on long voyages across the Atlantic and you'd never know," she explained. Not even the ladies' home section of the newspaper was allowed past the sentry, except in pre-shredded condition for papier mache projects in the occupational therapy room.

When a woman's sympathetic nervous system is out of alignment, when nothing can keep her blood from hovering and percolating around every nerve and muscle in her whole body, she must stay wide awake and fidget twenty-four hours a day. And the psychoactive stuff she's been prescribed tends to keep her brain sufficiently out of focus to prevent her from doing anything constructive to pass the time. So, what does this woman do--I mean, if she happens to be Mrs Sproul? She listens to AM radio.

And when she does that, it's not long before something becomes apparent: everything on the AM band, including the slips of the announcer's tongue, and even the bursts of static ostensibly caused by random flocks of sparrows caroming off antennas and so forth, is planned out in advance to achieve certain effects on the public mind.

Mrs Sproul figured out this halfway startling revelation with the collaboration of several paranoid-schizophrenic heroin addicts who lived down the hall. She got along well with this sort of youngster, having been a mother in the sixties.

They came up with the political overtones. Mrs Sproul herself didn't hear anything too specifically political, beyond America's default reactionary cretinism; but the various layers of programming did seem to dovetail more often than not, in a surreptitious kind of way. She suspected that a level of saturation such as those teenaged inmates received through their perpetually grunting rock stations might, in the end, alter one's behavior to fit certain unwholesome patterns.

Mrs Sproul was not just thinking of voting or buying patterns. Everybody knows that's the way ads work. She meant patterns of thinking, feeling, and even dreaming. The most blatant example was the outfit known as "500,000 Kilowatt Clear Channel KAMA, 960 on Your Radio Dial, Your People Station!"

In the deepest hours of the night, they aired Nite Caps, a horrifying phone-in program for old ladies. Since it occupied one of the few clear channels in the whole ionosphere, KAMA could be heard across a quarter of the earth's surface. The wretches were presumably calling from bedsitter flats, farm houses and rest homes scattered over every point in the United States, Canada and the

Kamchatka peninsula, for all I knew.

Mrs Sproul confessed that she hadn't yet figured out whether KAMA actually answered the phone and screened each caller for appropriate mood, subject matter and vocal quality, or whether they had a back room at the station, a sweatshop full of washed-up actresses stationed at big tables with scripts piled in front of them. The latter seemed more likely, to both of us, because every moment of Nite Caps flowed straight from the previous and into the next with a terrible logic. There was even a "rudimentary, if twisted, beauty to it," as she said, and as I found out for myself, at Mrs Sproul's insistence.

She recruited me to help monitor the situation. Like any regular junior high boy, I was eating grotesque amounts of blotter acid in those days, and sleeping about the same number of hours per night as my locked-up friend, so I was ideal for the job.

Mrs Sproul could sometimes arrange to be in hydrotherapy for the earlier stages of the program. It was easier to sneak a listen in the private bathroom than in the corridors. Before tuning in she must sit down in the long stainless steel sarcophagus and make sure that any sores or hangnails on her hands and feet were peeled open and bleeding. She'd always been this way, even before losing her mind officially. So her extremities were in pretty bad shape on a permanent basis. "A mass of carnage," she confessed. "But the rest of my body, well, that's a different matter."

Someone had given her a new two-piece especially for this visit to the loony bin. I never saw the garment, but I can tell you that it was light blue and very youthful. "Perhaps too youthful," she allowed, "though I haven't heard anybody complain yet."

Certain of the mood-altering substances she took were supposed to exacerbate water retention, but somehow Mrs Sproul had managed to escape scot free on that account. Her thighs were still firm and lumpless, even on top and in between, or so she claimed. It was evident, through the muu-muu that she sported in the community room, that Mrs Sproul's breasts had also stood up tolerably well. Noting my scrutiny, she pointed out that she'd never encouraged the flow of heavy cream by nursing Samuel, the expatriate clarinetist/lyric poet. (I got the strange impression that she hadn't held out on him by choice.)

This was a sort of cut-rate education for an unpopular teen like me, an extra-credit Health and Personal Hygiene class, so I stuck with her. She was willing to slip such an appreciative audience some of the brain pills that were supposed to be swallowed after supper. They were pharmaceutical, of course, and cooked down nicely, and knocked me flat on my back, even as they bounced off the brick wall of my patroness' awareness like so many ping pong balls. She was downright chipper in the wee hours.

In the most anxiety-ridden moments of our linked lives, between one and three a.m., the Nite Caps discussion theme is disease and disintegration. In that time slot, the callers from Miami to Juneau to Baja, California, all seem to want to talk about their dying husbands, just by coincidence, to vent intimations of mortality into the sleepy ears of literally millions of old ladies spread over a fourth of the planet. With each call the conversation gets more specific, until finally they're describing the threads of pajama flannel that dangle from the yellow crust oozing between the sutures over Grampy's last unsuccessful gall bladder operation. I don't know about my co-listener, but my brain chemistry at such moments enabled, or rather obliged, me to apprehend each of those flannel threads with all five senses, plus the esoteric sixth and seventh that obtain on the far side of the Himalayas, where folks used to guzzle the fabled Soma moon-juice, chemical ambition of every red blooded American teen-boy.

The callers at these times all have soft, vague voices designed to lull you into a hypnagogic state where your back-brain will be suffused with the odor of overripe flesh, and you'll be deathly-relaxed, misty, suggestible and defenseless against the three-a.m. top-of-the-hour climax.

For a good long while Mrs Sproul has been staring up at the little terrycloth drapes over the chicken wired window. Somebody has taken the time and trouble to brush the outer threads of the tiny orange tassels, to make them look fine and silken instead of coarsely wound. Between its pastel-enameled bars, this window affords a view--if you stand on tip-toe, pull the drapes aside, and peer through a certain un frosted streak in the glass--of the Capital Casino. I believe Mrs Sproul, but only in the anagogical sense, when she claims that jingling dump was a favorite hangout in her pre-loony bin days. "AM radio in three dimensions," she used to call it. "KAMA for the nose, eyes and tongue."

There seemed to be a house rule in the Capital Casino's coffee shop that one had to make one's mouth look like pudenda when ordering "griddle cakes, tall stack." And one had to exchange rudimentary badinage and behave in seductive lesbian ways with the bleached waitress in her French parlor maid's outfit, her face powdered with all the arid lassitude of the Salt Flats, which began their crystalline creep just outside the kitchen door.

On the far side of the cinderblock walls of this den of iniquity are the defunct state penitentiary grounds. Zoned in rows along the former prison yard are motels-cum-legal brothels, green stucco. And bordering their crowded parking lots are the tumbleweeded airstrips where open-air hydrogen bomb delivery test flights took off in the fifties--one of which had her son's name on it.

"God didn't pull the boo-boo, Dear," she would sputter in Samuel's unhappy face during the difficult afternoons when she'd forgotten to renew her Aventyl prescription. She'd try to explain, in terms graspable to him, the hypothetical relationship between birth defects and nuclear radiation, because he'd come home crying about his specialty being ridiculed at kindergarten or junior high, or college, or whatever it was.

"The boo-boo was pulled by President Eisen--I mean, the Department of Defen--I mean, the foul fiend Flibbertigi--I mean, your mother--I mean, um, yes, Mother Nature. Mother Nature pulled the boo boo, Sammy. Not Heavenly Father."

The only reason she used to subject herself to the Capital Casino and griddle cakes, tall stack, was so she could be near those disused airstrips and remember, never forget the first moment she'd laid eyes on him languishing in the incubator, an unknown priest performing emergency baptism with distilled water through a glove box. The nose was split and flapping, the upper lip non-existent, the whole cherubic countenance hanging open like a red change purse, the eyes pressed up from the bloodless gash below: two blind mongoloid slits, like a Japanese baby's. A Nagasaki changeling had taken up residence in the maternity ward just downstairs from Mrs Sproul's present place of confinement.

Death is the word that had filled her skull, as the original sin of this small thing was rinsed down Our Lady of Sorrows' drain. From the outer tegument of her cerebral cortex to the reptilian crannies of her lower brain stem: death.

When you've been thoroughly reminded of your own frailty, Nite Caps brings on the vampires who sound as though they've given up the fight against senility, and left off trying to maintain even a modicum of personal dignity. The insinuation is that such behavior represents the only alternative to morbid pining for the superannuated female.

These seniors cackle at non-existent jokes, they babble

happily, they play their worm-eaten Color Glo organs into the telephone and sing "Whoa Promise Me." As soon as they're sure you've been jolted wide awake by their racket, these goofy crones suddenly get serious. They lose their speech impediments as if by magic and become coherent as the shrewdest demagogue. They start making loud jingoist comments about this international sisterhood, this Nite Caps Radio Network, this invaluable service performed for the elderly, the infirm, the insomniac, the acid-adled.

And here Nite Caps abandons all pretense of unrehearsedness. Someone in the studio switches on a tape player, and the whole northwestern quadrisphere of Gaia Terra segues into a stirring rendition of the famous Nite Caps Anthem.

Meanwhile, inside the Capital Casino, Panguitch, Nevada, someone on a wobbling stepladder vacuums among unstitched pleats in meat-colored velvet that drapes the unlit stage and the holy-of holies beyond. Nearby, the blackjack dealer in a tiny halter-top stands like an unsuccessfully galvanized corpse, so long-dead that its age must match its weight. Bits of green baize adhere to its forearms like crypt-mold. The change maker, her nickel-plated coin dispenser wedged horizontally between rolls of sebaceous cellulite, stalks the gamblers like a bloated returnee from a salt water drowning. The Keno balls rattle like bones in their cages. An aging prostitute behind the bar breathes hoarsely into her microphone and, drones a lipsticky invocation:

"Mo Katz. Phone call. Mo Katz."

Mrs Sproul's ex-doctor might barge in at any moment, let there be no doubt. That's the only reason she even bothers to wear her light-blue two piece in the private bathroom--though he isn't supposed to come anywhere near the locked ward because he's nobody's doctor anymore (a small matter of malpractice and license suspension).

Her ex-doctor breaches the gate periodically because his sole purpose in life these days is to weasel a certain piece of information out of Mrs Sproul. She doesn't have this information, but pretends she does and is willfully withholding it from him, because she likes to see how many different ways he can figure to finagle his way into the ward. She is amused by the sullen yet amazed way I stare at the stumpy little shrink, and it's fun for both of us to hear the burly orderlies eject him.

Sometimes, before coming right out and demanding to be enlightened, her ex-doctor will try to soften her up with a brief discussion of something he presumes to be high-level, such as psychoanalytic theory (still an issue out here among the social climbing upper-middle classes on the far left fringe of the heartland). Not many literate people are locked up this time around, and he assumes that she must be starving for some elevated discourse. She's not; she has Nite Caps.

Whenever her ex-doctor brings up his only field of expertise, she interrupts him and speaks dismissively of You-Know-Who. She says, through a yawn, "A bit parochial, don't you think? Like his emphasis on this Oedipal thing. Certainly not applicable to every single one of the families I've seen in my day. It's not a system of thought I'd want to devote my entire life to."

Of course, this is calculated to infuriate a self respecting biological Freudian, who nevertheless cannot prevent himself from being traumatized by even the offhanded opinions of a woman shapely as Mrs Sproul. He blurts out something like, "We'll see what Samuel has to say about that."

Rather than hear this profane grotesquery take her son's name in vain, Mrs Sproul makes bold to disconnect her earplug and turn up the volume, to drown out the nasal whine. As if on cue, the Mormon Tabernacle Choir comes on howling a monstrous jingle.

> *We're the Nite Caps, nighty-Nite Caps,*
> *And our hearts are full of cheer!*
> *We love our Nite Caps radio show,*
> *But most of all we love to hear*
> *The voice of our own Herb Jebco!*

This is followed by a come-on for the next Nite Caps Convention, with cut-rate accommodations offered at Howard Johnson's, just down the block. "Under the sign of the H & J!"

Herb Jebco is the originator and organizer and host of all this, a faceless man with flawless enunciation, who must've done something terrible to his mother, since he felt the need to devise such an elaborate act of penance. "Maybe Herb put her in the loony bin, too," suggests Mrs Sproul's ex-doctor in a reptilian hiss. The hollow fangs find their mark, as I can tell when all the blood drains from her face via the jugular, and leaves this woman looking her age (for the moment).

She knows very well, without a stumpy half-man insinuating it into her ear, that she is a spiteful woman. So full of floating spite, which finally found an object when she came to these parts long ago and encountered the pithecoid locals and their amusements.

But Samuel was able to gestate, more or less, and ripen among them, as one of them, in one of their radioactive strongholds, and was happy, and only left the state, the continent, to avoid seeing his mother disintegrate in the attic of Our Lady of Sorrows Hospital-- from whose porch you can see, through sturdy chain-links, the giant H & J glowing orange and turquoise over the downtown sidewalk.

Thousands of washed-up widows, including some of Mrs Sproul's fellow inmates, believe it to signify Herb Jebco. There are times when even I forget who is which, and reach for my radio dial upon feeling a sudden conditioned hankering to take advantage of the fried clam-strip luncheon special--not so much to eat it as to examine it closely in horror, and see if it makes a noise anywhere near as hideous as a defrocked brain-priest breaking down and raving his real reason for being where he's not supposed to be:

"What's your god-damned son saying about me in his insane songs?"

Awash in his own counter-transference, facing permanent revocation of his license, and still making threats when Samuel's clear across the ocean in the UK.

Wait a minute. In the UK?

As Mrs Sproul mechanically shreds hands and feet in the endless water, she returns to her vague presentiment.

No, not a presentiment. She didn't used to have such bad reality testing before this clear-channel business. She remembers now that it was something tangible, an out-and-out palpable piece of writing, that told her in so many words: Samuel's coming home soon.

Yes, a young dope addict got it for her. A pitiful, pimply boy infatuated with "Mrs S" stole it off the supervisor's desk. It was a Trafalgar Square postcard with pigeons and things.

You do eventually get to see your picture postcards here at Our Lady of Sorrows, but only after the supervisor obliterates the back with blue ink. The sweet little junkie, as part of his youthful protest against being confined in the sensory deprivation chamber last week, stole this postcard before obliteration, and smuggled it in to her along with the transistor radio, his tribute to "Mrs S" upon whom he has a crush.

And that's the explanation for this presentiment mix-up. She must've been under the influence of the devil's own thorazine at the moment these gifts were delivered. She must've been mixing her senses, and hearing her perfect genius ideal boy's written words, as from the mouth of a radio deejay: "I am coming home soon," looped goofily among the regular back-of-the-postcard unctuousness, and Paul Harvey's page two.

All those hours of amplitude modulation. Analyzing it to clarify a non-existent presentiment. For nothing!

Then it hits her again: Samuel's coming home soon, raised to a much higher level of certainty than mere presentiment now. She has an exhilarating access of fondness for her perfect genius ideal boy. Samuel's coming home soon, and her sudden mania of biochemical affection spills out upon the whole of society, like the sun rising over North America. It makes the gray snowfields on the distant mountainsides glint like aluminum siding. Alarm clocks go off in bedroom communities scattered along the rectilinear borderlands, and Mrs Sproul's mood switches again, as one or another of the several chemicals inside of her--the lithium, the Librium, the Aventyl--sloshes to another cranny of cranial molecules. KAMA obliges her by nailing the lid on the weird sisters for the next twelve hours, and supplanting them (at least until the sun sinks again) with the clicking, blipping weather and stock market reports, ads for transmission fluid, Roto Rooter; parched horizontal static, busy snips of people chanting or mumbling into the electronic desert; UPI World Desk International, Ray Conniff Singers--red roses for a blue, blue lady.

Mrs Sproul's affection floats inward. She feels genuine, sweet, inner piety. She doesn't loathe Herb Jebco at all any more. She will go mad with remorse here in the long steel coffin. Remorse for having been so spiteful. Such a floatingly spiteful woman.

When she was just a girl her family disintegrated with the world economy, and she was sent out here to the convent school, against her will. It was her first experience with a part of the country where people generically called themselves Christians--no denomination, just Christians. They'd congregate in the wilderness for weekend retreats and baptize each other in milky-green drainage ditches. She would sit alone in the convent and consider those hicks with glee, and pray to Mary for one of those screaming salt rainstorms: "Mother of Christ, bring it rolling in across the desert!" She'd imagine sometimes that she was up in the clouds, pissing down on everybody in a yellow torrent.

She wanted more than anything to be in a tornado--even one of these half-hatched tramontane ones would do. She'd sit by the big wireless in the refectory with a county map in her lap, plotting along with the announcer the course of any funnel clouds that touched down. She could feel everyone's eardrums pressing out from within, and all their clothes pulled off, everybody naked, screaming and flying from the terror and the suck, the nearly flawless "O" of wind forming an almost perfect seal with Earth's yielding surface, and bringing up cows, calves, whole stands of utility poles that bristled like Saint Sebastian with embedded alfalfa stalks.

Samuel's coming home soon. Yes, she has this vague feeling in her bones, like a presentiment. She somehow knows: soon she and Samuel will be sharing a continent.

Riding the Horse

Our educational policy must enable everyone who receives an education to develop morally, intellectually and physically.
Quotations of Chairman Mao

Hong Ma Han, the formidable Red Horseman, was living almost exactly as he had as a junior middle school student before the mobilization. But Bu Yu immediately noticed some important differences.

Today it was Hong Ma Han who occupied the sitting room, while his parents stayed mostly in the tiny side room. And today thick black curtains hung over the windows to prevent the bright, unsmoky sunshine, the immemorial boast of this mountain town, from obscuring the picture on Hong Ma Han's brand new television set.

The last time Bu Yu had ridden through on a linkup, televisions, even black and white ones, and certainly color Japanese imports like this, were unheard of. But now nearby Black Flower Mountain boasted a new silver skeleton of a pagoda that brought education to Hong Ma Han. He was one of a totally new breed of Chinese: a television university student.

It was said that Daoist clergy and monastics in the hills had taken to worshipping that relay tower, and it didn't exactly represent a benevolent god to them.

Another difference in the Red Horseman's life was the large carton of expensive western-style toilet paper, perfumed, and rolled instead of folded, that came close to vying with the television as the focus of attention in this small apartment.

"What's all the pink paper for?"

Hong Ma Han mumbled something elusive about getting it at a discount from his father's dan wei, and let it pass.

Bu Yu's former comrade-in-arms obviously never set foot outdoors any longer. He was almost as colorless as the pink-eyed "false foreigners" one used to see in freak shows in the late fifties, before the provincial governor read some contraband books, became influenced by western humanistic ideals and decided that albinos should be gainfully employed in photographic film factories. Hong Ma Han, once a mighty warrior, seemed afraid now of going out. But, oddly, he also seemed happy—too happy, in fact. He giggled at the slightest provocation.

"My father's unit is paying for all of this," he said. "I have some good guanxi now. If I stay home and don't flunk the mail-order test, I'll be the first person from this town to get an academic certificate since Shui Shui Bo the bandit sat for the imperial examinations disguised as a bourgeois landlord."

Hong Ma Han embraced himself and giggled—unnaturally, it seemed to Bu Yu.

"And how soon will you graduate?"

More than seven years Hong Ma Han had reputedly lingered in front of the screen, yet it seemed as though that question had never occurred to him. His face went limp a few seconds, his eyes dead, like someone with slight epilepsy. He sucked his lips gently, like a baby, and seemed only half-conscious for a couple of seconds.

His mother brought in something made almost entirely of sugar and grease, apparently as a snack. No hot meal had produced itself yet.

"You have a good mother," said Bu Yu.

"She's nothing compared to yours," whispered Hong Ma Han, looking furtively over the back of his armchair. He seemed about to continue on the same subject, but glanced at Bu Yu and, with an audible gasp, stopped talking. Bu Yu must've sunken his fingernails into his forehead in torment, for the Red Horseman shied off and steered the conversation away from mothers.

"Tell me more about your brother. Why is he going to a university so obscure, and so full of counterrevolutionaries and democracy demonstrators?"

"You know the answer to that question," said Bu Yu.

In his urgency to explain Younger Brother's inexplicable life, Bu Yu didn't fully register the mention of student demonstrators, except as a vague thrill in his stomach. It was the first he'd heard of this. But they demonstrated in the name of democracy, not something better and more real. So perhaps they weren't worth notice.

"You know the answer," repeated Bu Yu, and he began working his hands in the air, groping for words among the rotten memories.

In an attempt to create an incident that would attract the attention of the central authorities, Bu Yu's united-faction brigade had gotten carried away in "dragging out" and struggling the wife of the provincial foreign affairs minister. This reactionary politician had immediately afterwards gotten himself transferred to America, far enough away to avoid further patriotic scrutiny by the Red Guards, so he'd been able to remain in power after the smoke cleared. The result was that each member of Bu Yu's brigade had been hounded and persecuted without mercy for the past ten years, except for the ones with powerful fathers. Bu Yu's father, as a pile of ashes in an urn on the side of a mountain, had little power to spare.

Bu Yu had been internally exiled. But, since the family line would have died out with him, the widowed minister had mercifully allowed Younger Brother, only a child at the time Madame Minister was fatally violated with the adze blade, to return to town after just a few years under the Shifu's charge. But, of course, only the worst university in the province seemed to have a slot for him.

"A sad story," said Hong Ma Han, whose brigade had stayed safe in this town during that period, willing prisoners of mothers who wouldn't allow their children the glory of pulling down the highest provincial officials.

"And this elephant-sized foreign specialist," continued Hong Ma Han after the appropriate moment of silence, "the only one who would teach in such a piss-pot because I'm sure he's a criminal or derelict—you say he persecutes Xiao Bu?"

"Mosquito Lunch he calls him. In my commune—er, not mine, but—"

Hong Ma Han terrifiedly giggled something about being assimilated into the peasant stratum. Bu Yu spoke louder.

"—they still hold firm the memory of Mao's little red dragons at Pao An who aided so resolutely in the struggle against—"

Trying to help, Hong Ma Han finished the sentence with gibberish, as if to say, "Yes, yes, please go on."

"Mao's men didn't call their youth insect names," said Bu Yu. "They said Comrade to one another, and meant it."

"Yes, I suppose they did, didn't they?" said Hong Ma Han, obviously thinking of something else. He eyed his watch. "Say, when you leave here, I know a place you can go where you might find help. You can drop in on the Black Flower Temple, near the relay tower, in fact. Before the CCTV construction team cut the road up there, that temple was considered quite remote. Too remote for our little generals to bother sacking it during the Four Olds campaign. So I assume they're still in operation. And that's lucky for you, because you must cross Black Flower Mountain eventually, mustn't you?"

When Bu Yu didn't jump right up and start climbing cliffs, Hong Ma Han looked at his watch again, and decided to try to tantalize his guest further.

"Do you know any card or coin tricks? Or maybe something with stick matches? Do something like that for the nuns and they'll kowtow to you as the latest reincarnation of the Buddha and let you eat the boiled breasts of their white chickens. At night you can sleep on the altar and gorge on the jungle people's fruit offerings, if you can manage to gag down the incense ash they're covered with. The nuns will greet the day thinking the Black Flower Mountain spirits have eaten well, and they'll praise you, pray to you and feed you more chicken because your presence is appetizing to the local ghosts."

During all this talk about food, Hong Ma Han kept rubbing his belly and licking his cheeks and the base of his nose. Bu Yu didn't remember his tongue being this long. Then the smile left his face and he got serious.

"But you'll have to clear out in a couple days or so, because the last time somebody tried this—a purged member of our outfit, as a matter of fact, who got lost in the dark and had to sleep outside a few nights—the mother superior sent a fleet-footed messenger to the party secretary at Zhengxin. She's always held out the hope of converting him and, through him, I suppose, the party apparatus of the whole county. And what better way than to introduce him to the magic sleight-of-hand Buddha himself? And, of course, the secretary sent up a couple militiamen to arrest the boy for fraud. Nobody's seen him since."

Hong Ma Han's voice trailed off as he realized that last anecdote might be a little discouraging. He picked up his line of thought at an earlier point.

"Before you go down off the mountain, you can lift one of the tape recorders the nuns conduct funeral services with, automatic praying machines to preserve their devout throats for swallowing the bereaved family's food and wine. They're cheap domestic goods, nothing Japanese yet—unless the nuns've been experiencing a boom in business with the open-door policy. But they'll bring you a few kuai in town among the suburbanite peasant classes."

The Red Horseman glanced back to make sure his mother wasn't in the room, then leaned forward and whispered, "I've been told there's this one simple-minded novice-type nun whose delicate meat you can enter—"

When Bu Yu reacted with open shock and disgust, Hong Ma Han retreated and said, "Yes, it is terrible, isn't it? But you always were a reformist in that respect, too."

"And more than one boy in your contingent had a terrible

reputation."

Inevitably, they'd begun reopening old factional wounds. The situation was now even more hopeless than before. Bu Yu was ready to weep like a girl with fatigue and loneliness and disappointment.

The Red Horseman seemed to sense the crisis. "So, what did you expect from me?" he asked in a quieter voice. He gazed at Bu Yu's bare, bleeding feet, at the cuts and bruises that only served to stoke Bu Yu's revolutionary ardor. It wouldn't be as easy to get rid of him as Hong Ma Han supposed.

"Come with me and help," said Bu Yu.

"I must stay here and study," he murmured, not even convincing himself. "Deng Xiaoping has urged us to be both red and expert."

"But you are—we called you the Red Horseman. The mighty Hong Ma Han. Don't you remember? All by yourself you conducted reconnaissance work for the Putian incident when our detachments were locked up bleeding in the P.L.A. stockade."

"Exactly. Do you realize how close I came to being killed?"

"Yes? Well? All of us, several times, came close to—"

"Don't you understand?" Hong Ma Han raked the air over his viscera with his fingernails. He peered past the edge of the television into the black corners of his parents' apartment. "I was all by myself that night. Do you know what I mean? Alone."

For a full minute, Bu Yu stared wordlessly at this lone Chinaman.

"Please don't have contempt for me," whispered Hong Ma Han.

"I don't think I do. Really, I don't think so."

The Red Horseman looked back into the glowing colors of the screen for a moment, absorbed, mustering his emotional forces.

"I have an idea," he said. "Stop me if you think I'm being reactionary or something."

He went to a chest of drawers and got out his old arm band and Mao quotations. He handed Bu Yu something to place over the heart inside his breast: one of the red lapel pins which airplane factories used to produce instead of airplanes back in the sixties. He embarrassed Bu Yu further by dragging out an old ragged portrait of the Great Helmsman. Just as Bu Yu hoped he wouldn't do, he began to chant and sway: it was the loyalty dance that Bu Yu thought he'd never see again in China. This was preparatory to the random opening of the Little Red Book, to receive words to live by, the day's directive.

Hong Ma Han looked, and read solemnly: "Quit your farting."

He squealed, giggled, hugged himself, seemingly transported; but all the while he was examining the dial of his watch through the tears of forced mirth that slid like temple balm down his rice-colored cheeks.

"You'll have to excuse me, Comrade, ah, Bu. It's time for my French class. The teacher is excellent, merci beaucoups, a lovely overseas Chinese girl."

He turned the television up, then ushered Bu Yu out into the concrete stairwell in a splash of rats.

Before the door closed Hong Ma Han could be seen unrolling whole meters of scented pink tissue onto his left hand and settling himself into the overstuffed chair he'd liberated from his father.

The Red Horseman's mother tiptoed to pull the black drapes more tightly shut.

Proving Grounds

My solitude grew more and more obese, like a pig.
Yukio Mishima

When things were normal, Mr. Fukuoka could be found trying to teach Japanese to rich teenagers in a prep school in the mountainous north. But, tonight being abnormal, he found himself in the southern wastes, visiting the scene of a crime perpetrated against him when his was younger than his students, when he was known as Little Flip.

Wandering off alone into raucous blackness, Mr. Fukuoka fell, humbled, to pray, upon the abrasive desert floor, and impaled both knees on a decaying coil of War Relocation Authority barbed wire. Peeling that up from the sterile dust, he discovered an intact jar, its glass blued by decades of ultraviolet radiation, its label bleached but legible. No mayonnaise, but the crispy remains of two baby rattlesnakes were visible inside, greened by jaundiced moonlight.

Little Flip had intended to domesticate them, or at least to save them from the bullsnakes (long, thick, and black as the donkey penises cited in the Book of Ezekiel) which the guards had been ordered to set loose on the periphery to chase the mother rattlers off. But he had either forgotten or, more likely, in his dispossessed state, had lacked the means, to punch air holes in the lid. Dried macaroni-like mummies with microscopic fangs were the result of his lifetime's sole visitation by the nurturing instinct, active or passive.

"Better known as Hellman's Real Mayonnaise east of the Rockies, which is where you rice-niggers should be," a bully guard had mumbled. Physically unfit for combat, bug-eyed and hoarse, the guard had tried to confiscate the jar, but had been persuaded to relent by a golden and blue angel from the mountains.

"A child needs his pets," the Mormon missionary had smirked. "Just as we grownups do."

Tonight, shaking the concentration camp relic in his hand like a baby rattle or sorcerer's fetish, Mr. Fukuoka found himself stumbling down a dry gully and into a roaring corner of red-sand Topheth. He peeked between a cactus' upthrust fists; and what he saw stunned and paralyzed him like a double injection of hot reptile venom. He froze, obscured in lurching campfire shadows. He seemed to have almost walked in on a Canaanite orgy.

The throbbing explosions could have been his own heart imploding, self-destructing in waltz rhythm; the screams and profanities and flashes and tracers could have been his eyeballs and eardrums bursting out of heir appointed seats, being washed away, dislodged by the sheer pressure inside his head; the artificial winds could have shot from the four dilated nostrils of a yoke of supernal Palmyra oxen bearing on each of their backs one foot of the awful Bedouin Yahweh, come to deliver the final revelation of all time.

A detachment of jeering junior shamans, lithe and semi-clothed Caucasoid apprentices to red masters, howled and brawled among themselves with broad gestures. They sent forth bolts of lurid fire from their bony, outstretched arms and into Heaven's black midsection. Boys' lean backs and buttocks were plainly visible. Sinewy creatures, seemingly one-armed, followed behind them and whispered abominable jokes over their shoulders and into their juvenile ears, hunching and huffing very close, making the centaur with seven limbs.

He should have suspected something in homeroom the week before.

The polygamist children from the boarding department had reacted so jubilantly to the geology teacher's proposal of a geode-digging "all-nighter" among nerve-gassed sheep carcasses in the U. S. Army's proving grounds. Japanese language instructor to the children of the nouveaux riches for an entire week already, Teachie-poo-sensei had assumed, in his naivete, that the Lord was giving him a chance to teach these privileged white children a connotation of the word topaz other than the one found at position eight of Professor Moh's unrevised, unexpanded Hardness Scale, which the geology teacher kept tacked to the homeroom wall. At the very top of the chart, just above diamond, someone phenomenally tall had penciled a new position of ultimate hardness: "Nip homo boners."

It had been part of his new-on-the-job hazing to be duped by the other faculty members into co-chaperoning this field trip. He could have had no idea what he was in for; could never have imagined what white teens were capable of.

"What does our right-honorable governor call that county?" one of them had squealed from the back row of desks.

"Panoramaland!" the rest of them had hooted in unison, making googly-eyes and whirling their index fingers in psychedelic spirals around each other's ears.

"Our patriarchal stomping grounds!" the polygamist children

had screeched. (The administration let anybody with lots of money into the school.) "Time to take care of some business, boys!"

And here was the reason for their jubilation.

Instead of the sand-dune Jehovah's sublime voice, the youngish Japanese teacher heard the scratchy squawks of adolescent heathens of only near-angelic physique. When not dancing like naked dervishes in the firelight, they seemed to be hawking various survivalist paraphernalia and ordnance freshly delivered, in the original factory boxes, from the belly-hatch of their millionaire patriarch's helicopter.

The shoppers appeared to be Marxist bucks and savage septuagenarian peyotists from the Shivwit tribe aboriginal to this smoking cranny of Gehenna. They'd been latterly elevated to polite Intermountain society's upper-middle ranks by the discovery of lush uranium deposits on their reservation, plus generous federal recompenses for nerve agent leakages. They had shown up tonight not in the expensive sharkskin business suits they wore to New Zion's Bank, but in traditional buckskin sweat-lodge garb--a canny enough wardrobe choice, considering the fatuous young romantics they were dealing with. Their exquisitely beaded loincloths were bolstered plump with stumpy red penises and substantial wads of equally hard currency, neither of which they seemed particularly desirous of keeping a hold on.

For the native Americans' benefit, one of the less gifted Japanese students demonstrated something brand-new in those days: a surface-to-air, shoulder-deployed, heat-seeking anti-aircraft missile. The suggested target was a single crawling point of light far overhead which everybody surmised to be an Israeli spy satellite. And the rocket seemed, after a slithering, smoking chase through the constellations, to find its mark, filling the suborbital void with livid blasts of light, and the desert with incredulous howls of glee.

Cadets from the polygamist family's private military academy defiantly discharged their M16's, Uzis and AK-47's into Orion's belt, confident of their immunity from prosecution on this scofflaw reservation, where the bare mention of the words Bureau of Alcohol, Tobacco and Firearms could be relied upon to elicit hoots of derision from even the stoniest-faced old squaw.

Without being told, the youngish Japanese teacher somehow decided that he was witnessing nothing less than red communism cutting a deal with under-aged splinter Mormonism. They most likely were hatching a nefarious plot to stage a paramilitary coup in this county, at whose southernmost extreme was situated a vast dam that provided life-sustaining electricity to considerable portions of that militarily sensitive area known as the west coast of the United States of America.

Only minutes before, Teachie-poo-sensei had discreetly absented himself from the girls. They appeared to be camping more or less legitimately, if one ignored the mushroom clouds of hemp smoke belching from the turquoise mouths of their sleeping bags. He'd left those future brides of Satan under the chortling, geode-fondling supervision of the geology teacher ("Damn Army boys must be re-hearsin' for 'nother damn Tit Offensive out there on the damn provin' grounds!"), and he had scrambled deep into the moonlight. Almost insane with masochistic nostalgia for the relocation camp, and the guards, and the intrusive right hand of the golden and blue missionary, he had found nothing more edifying than an old vermin-rattling mayonnaise jar, and this mescaline Eucharist.

In the hot night air, hiding among the shadows at the rout's periphery, the youngish Japanese teacher found himself slipping into a delirium of rage at the sight of his boyhood's praying ground being desecrated by moneychangers, an intoxication compounded by furiously denied sexual arousal at the spectacle itself.

His heart began to swell with some half-formed intention of bringing fright and firepower to bear upon the pony-tailed socialists and the spawn of multiple fornication. He would drive them like sheep; he would force them to ooze their lubricious selves ten yards due west, or maybe twenty or thirty, or maybe a hundred miles, across sperm-yellow salt and scab-red sand, to where he hallucinated the county line. There, beyond the protection of the county attorney--who happened to be a plural mother of the "polygily-wiggly" boys--they would be forced to undergo citizen's arrest at the Japanese teacher's passion-quaking hands.

Quaking hands, but not bare.

Falling again to his punctured knees, he began to gather what he trusted were the raw ingredients of simple but effective explosive compounds. With splitting fingernails he scratched up various soils from his long-abandoned bridal bed, plus shirt-pocketsful of hardness-eight gravel to serve as splattergun projectiles. He prayed a weeping prayer of repentance as he performed the damnation offense of removing and shredding, for a fuse and wadding material, his official Church undergarments, this world's only sure prophylaxis from the black influence of Beelzebub. With adrenalin strength he wrenched the crumbling tailpipe from an abandoned army jeep, an orange barrel for this primitive but blessed blunderbuss.

Then he stumbled through the darkness and, mostly with his fingertips' sensitive skin, set about scrounging a sort of soldier-of-God uniform for himself, a disguise, improvised from dry stone detritus and desert carrion. He peeled some skin from a dead, pregnant ewe's jaws and eye sockets and stretched it across his own face to protect his lungs and brain cells from the toxic fumes of whatever burnt holocaust his pupils might be offering up to their Canaanite bull-god. With his bare teeth he gnawed free from their spindly anklebones the clawed feet of a gluttony-burst vulture, coated them with his own scant saliva and mud-pasted them to either side of his head: elfin ears, dead pinfeathers tickling. Like Moses himself, he sprouted a steer's parched and porous horns, and encircled them with a thorn-crown of blood-colored and blood-reeking barb wire.

As he made himself over, the gruesome elements in his costume began ever so gradually to be obscured by glistening ones: beads of sun-blued glass from coolies' shattered opium jars were draped from either earlobe; ivory-colored hair barrettes and false eyelashes were alluringly fashioned from baby rattlesnakes' filament-fine skeletons, lovingly shaken, with curled fifth fingers, out of the mayonnaise jar. And, in case his mask slipped, he concocted himself a facial foundation of talc-fine sand, wind-sifted, and moistened seductively with blood from his own tear-ducts. A powder of pollen was coaxed from cactus blooms clenched for the evening but finger-pried apart like moist fairy buttocks. And all this was obscured ever so subtly by a pagan bridal veil of woven cactus spines.

Heavenly Father's voice suddenly rang out from the hilly north. It blasted a passage through the night clouds and rebounded off the exposed depths of outerspace: "Leave off thy preening, effeminate son of the Gibeah Benjaminites! Set aside thy whorish adornments and step forth with thy flaming rod into the light!"

But the Japanese teacher was a tobacco-free Latter-Day-Saint. He had no match to detonate his cannon. He began to wail aloud, a keening sob of lamentation, bringing all eyes in the vicinity down upon him.

Matter-of-factly, with no hesitation and little or no registration of surprise, the demoniacs embraced the creature that came hiccoughing from the shadows. They took his makeshift weapon and politely stacked it, tepee-style, among a cache of other wartime exotica, not even snickering. They draped him all about with their skin, their acne pockmarks and syringe-holes serving the same gripping function as suction cups on squid tentacles, and they drew him into the party, just another knot in the parched tangle of aborted serpents.

"Just another Utah misfit," laughed a horribly familiar teen voice, "a hairless Edom fucked out of his birthright for a bowl of bean soup--or, in this case, a pan of stir-fried green veggies!"

Leather-faced grannies gathered and gnawed on the youngish teacher's Japanese fingers in some nameless atavistic behavior. They shoveled handfuls of a sage-flavored incense onto the campfire. They fed him strychnine-tufted cactus bulbs that popped his brain-skin like an overripe hymen, and they laughed, at first affectionately, then derisively, at his impotence and structural underdevelopment.

The Mesopotamian god-head sprouted several writhing strands of hair, became a five-snake medusa, not only fatal, but impossible to behold for any creature without two faces, the second able to see behind.

The familiar boy's suffocating presence could be felt more and more, like a creeping odor. He squatted in the shadows and wrote in the living flesh of the orange sand with a slip of barb wire--not his Japanese calligraphy exercises, but something else, specifically for the benefit of three Shivwit braves, who gaped, were appalled, who giggled and wept in rapture and terror, who periodically touched one another's scaly elbows for corroborative witness, and manipulated their feathered fetishes to ward off the strong medicine contained in the overwhelming strokes that the white hand produced and wiped away with equal nonchalance.

"C'mon, you guys, can't you maintain twenty seconds in a row? These are the kind of questions they put on the entrance exam. Take 'em home to little Pocahontas, so she can come pitch her wigwam in our boarding department. We need some new blood around that dump."

At some rough jostle of a mighty sandstone elbow, very close to home, Teachie-poo-sensei was unmasked as he squatted and grimaced in a mound of ritually and literally defiled salt. Teacher and students' faces met: they grinned cougar teeth, flashed coyote tongues.

The brat's prematurely bleary eyes focused in a single direction for the first and last time. They lingered with impertinence where they shouldn't; but eventually those eyes managed to find their way around to the empty mayonnaise jar still clutched to the front of Teachie-poo-sensei's body, thence all the way up to his face.

In a convulsion of sheer delight, Sammy Edwine belched words destined to remain immemorial among the students of the Episcopalian college preparatory institution:

"Why, if it isn't Mr. Fuck You, Okay?"

Capitalist Roader

The Pope! How many divisions has he got?
Joseph Stalin

Bu Yu was standing right in front of the most dangerous place in town: the Public Security Bureau lockup. His legs had seized up at the knees and would convey him no further; so he began to try to pass the time of day with the People's Liberation Army men at the gate, hoping small talk would somehow allay their suspicions as to his motives for loitering in such a sensitive spot.

At first they just glanced at him and tried to brush him off like a dung beetle. But his persistence gradually began to embarrass them. The longer he insisted on sticking around, the likelier it became that someone whose opinion they valued, an inexpensive whore, perhaps, or the cadre in charge of their promotions--or any sentient adult at all, for that matter (these urbanites had an inflamed sense of face, living so crowded together)--might come along and mistake this madman for an associate of theirs.

So they dragged him, locked legs and all, into the guardhouse. They slammed the door and commenced interrogating him. He could barely hear his own replies over the barbarian music grunting from their tape machine.

"So what do you want from us?"

"Just exactly what I've been saying I want all along: to visit the lockup."

"He's a Taiwanese spy."

"He's a beggar from Anhui. He has no little brother but hunger. He wants to sneak in and pass himself off as an inmate so he can enjoy the delicious food we serve here."

"Yes, for example the chao fan with peanuts and prawns."

"And the shredded pork-stuffed pancakes in Sichuan pepper sauce."

Seeing these phrases produce an effect on neither his salivary glands nor the pupils of his eyes, the green men became a little more serious.

"This is not just an empty rice bucket we have here. There's something more inside him than a digestive tract."

They began to brandish their automatic weapons in his face.

"We could kill him right now and rid the workers of another

social parasite and nobody would be angry with us. He obviously has no mother to weep and wedge her flopping breasts between the gratings of our gate."

"No mother but foul crotch-odor."

"But I know someone who would be angry with us: the dogs. There'd be nobody from whose face to lick the pus-curds and rat shit late at night."

"Screw the dogs. Let's kill him now."

"But wait. Haven't we been instructed in political study meeting that no real beggars are left in our glorious Republic? Just millionaires in disguise, who glean entire cart-loads of foreign exchange currency from guilt-ridden overseas Chinese tourists. This Anhui beggar probably owns a five-room mansion with indoor plumbing, situated picturesquely upon several acres of fertile drainage plain outside town. He's a fraud, playing upon the natural sympathy of the yellow race and spoiling the appearance of our modernization with his filthy presence! Will we shoot him now and let him pass so painlessly through the gate to class-enemy Hell?"

"Certainly not. These capitalists fear dispossession a thousand times more than death. He must leave a little something as security before we allow him to take his natural rest with the executees."

"Do you have any trinkets, Stinky? Any relics? They're all over town, and I'd like a little something to take to my sweetheart on Flower and Willow Lane. Perhaps some jewels sprinkled from the dynastic titties of Empress Wu Zetian on one of her fabled pleasure-jaunts to our humble streets, time gone by?"

Bu Yu smiled and asked, "Is your sweetheart a philatelist?"

The butt-end of a rifle smashed into his temple.

"How dare you say such nasty things about a sweet girl you haven't even met yet?"

One of the comrades somehow managed to stop laughing long enough to define the term while Bu Yu applied pressure to the redness jetting from the side of his head.

"I have some wonderful ancient stamps," said Bu Yu, "from before Liberation."

"Elder Brother burned those in the Four Olds Movement, and we're still not allowed to do anything with them but turn them in."

"That's exactly why they're so very valuable. See?"

Bu Yu pulled a fat envelope from his decaying tunic. To his horror, many of the stamps had fused and melted together in his sweat and blood. He could do nothing but try to deceive these ignorant young men.

"I have one here from America. Triple-thick paper and special asymmetrical shape, see? It's what they call modern art, the decadent way the colors run together. That's the American Chairman Nikison when he was a field marshal collaborating with the Nationalist forces in Shaanxi against the Japanese aggressors. This was before the White Army split with us."

They looked skeptical.

"Why doesn't that horse he's sitting on have a barbecue-spit jammed up its ass and out its throat, like all its brothers in those days up north?"

Bu Yu made himself look shocked. "Didn't you know the Americans airlifted entire cavalry regiments to Shaanxi in 1928? And didn't you know the flesh of U.S. horses is poison, due to their being fed Negro babies twice a day? I thought everybody who'd been to middle school and paid attention knew that."

"Dog farts. This clown is having fun with us. Time to say zaijian."

Someone smashed the muzzle of a gun into Bu Yu's temple and pulled the trigger.

The soles of his feet rocketed into the roof of his skull, his kneecaps and entrails dragging behind in a ragged red stream. It was a sensation he hadn't felt in fifteen years or more: the self-inflicted agony of anticipated automatic weapon-fire that never came. It had to be worse than the real thing because it left a memory of the horror. The rapid, impotent clicks of the firing pin in the empty chamber and the cackles of the guards penetrated Bu Yu's scrambled brain cells, and came to his consciousness transformed into words.

* * * *

You can storm the provincial party headquarters. Please do. Attack the army and kill as many of them as you wish and steal their weapons. Burn the police stations. Detain, interrogate, torture the militiamen. Nobody will fight back. Would you care for a guided missile or two, just to speed things along? It's right there, for those of you courageous and clever enough to outwit its tenders.

But don't go near the broadcasting stations or you will be shot on sight.

It wasn't until these words came back to him that Bu Yu realized why his legs had seized up in front of this guardhouse: the radio station compound was just beyond. It was sentried in these relatively placid, bourgeois times by a single machine gun. Two decades before, if not for that immemorial injunction from on high, the little man behind the weapon wouldn't have caused a second's hesitation to a junior middle school auxiliary unit of Red Guards. But today Bu Yu had been unable to do anything but pretend to flirt with these Public Security Bureau maniacs next door.

And it took a physical act of will to prevent himself from remembering certain words somebody had once uttered which tarnished and cheapened the golden years of his life as a teen revolutionist. Once the will drained away, as it had been doing more and more readily over the past couple of weeks, the voice inside his head screeched out to him:

"Rebellion is made over the airwaves. But you so-called little generals don't dare attack the broadcasting station for fear of incurring the obese wrath of your Beijing god. You are not true revolutionaries at all, but mere dupes of the power structure. You are nothing more than unwitting royalist dogs!"

The sneering harangue was not a demon's, but possibly it was a ghost's. It was the voice of someone who not only hadn't memorized the Little Red Book as security against being cornered and quotationized, but had used wads of its pages as sanitary napkins, and referred to its author as "that wife's-ass licking cuckold." It was the voice of someone who'd met her end (death, detention, nobody seemed to know) singlehandedly storming that very radio station in her righteous, screaming "church militant" persona: Christ, judge of the quick and the dead, motherly mercy evaporatedaway, demolishing a temple full of moneychangers. The papist missionaries, if they hadn't been thrown out of China long ago, would have been shocked at what she grew into.

Bu Yu remembered the picture she'd hung on the mantle in place of the gentle Madonna and child, which had in its time replaced the ancestor-worship portrait of her mother's father's mother. It was a color reproduction of the back wall of a famous church in Italy, showing a beardless, bloated, red haired Christ, howling and grunting on his judgment seat, riding roughshod over the bad elements and class enemies of declining feudal Tuscan society: God rampant, smashing the masses with his left hand.

Her voice jeered at him, "No wonder every Chinese has rebuked your memory. You left your own father to be humiliated to death, you selfish, power-lustful, unfilial boy, no longer my son."

The scolding bitch-voice, reactivated after two decades of silence by Bu Yu's reentry into the environs of this horrible town, had once again made him feel like less than nothing, more than alone: annihilated.

But it had defeated its own purpose. He'd been purified of his own trivial self, even to the point where he occasionally lost his balance as he walked. Leaning on food stalls, shoulders and soot-filthy buildings, he'd finally become ready, worthy of paying a visit to the born moralist, stern Younger Brother, Mama's better boy, in Hell.

* * * *

"Don't they allow you boys cartridges for your clips?" asked Bu Yu very sweetly, before the guard's finger had even left the trigger.

The sounds that issued from the P.L.A. men's mouths were exactly midway between gasps and laughs.

His personality ripped away, Bu Yu was incapable of flinching. Instead, he clowned, put on false earnestness and spouted ridiculous philatelic lies, knowing that these boys, with their mind-numbing disco music, were his moral equals: just bored and soulless dupes of the various modernizations. They were grateful to the bringer of a laugh, any laugh that punctuated their deadly day and distracted them from the chilling suck of the ideological vacuum in which they were compelled to live out their lives. The identity he felt with these young men was adulterated by an ever so faint sensation, a soft echo of contempt, even as he accepted the favor of being let in the back way.

"You're on your own from here," they told him. "Go around the back, and if a jailer stops you, it would be better if you slashed your own throat, for here they do it very slowly with a dull, serrated blade."

Someone slipped him a razor, and asked for its return on the way out.

Bu Yu quietly dropped it behind some overflowing garbage dumpsters and approached the building toward which the glorious bronze Mao in the city square was holding out its hand: a yellow and turquoise facade, the color of new syphilis chancres on the sugar cane-fed buttocks of cash-crop cultivators. He went around to the loading dock and, using his own dirt as camouflage, slithered down into the sub-basement detention area.

In a single dark cell, swimming in piss, shit, blood, sperm and the less identifiable juices of at least one dead body, were twenty people, and Xiao Bu was among them, naked. He looked straight at his big brother but didn't seem to recognize him.

"I'm a barefoot doctor, come in from the communes to check you out," whispered Bu Yu, tentatively reaching his hands between the bars.

"No you're not," said Xiao Bu absently. "The barefoot doctors all returned to town ten years ago to become quacks and entrepreneurs." His throat sounded very dry, and he seemed unable to focus his eyes, but he didn't draw back from Elder Brother's touch.

Younger Brother had not been seriously interrogated yet. Bu Yu could tell from the chaotic distribution of the cuts, bruises and welts across his little body, and from the crush-type fractures that deformed his wrists, nose and rib cage. These were mob injuries, probably inflicted by his captors, mere street amateurs. It was not the "tight bombing pattern" that P.S.B. interrogators prided themselves on, which they'd developed as Red Guards struggling their middle school teachers. Bu Yu had seen, suffered and inflicted enough of both kinds of wounds to be able to tell the difference at a glance. Sometimes he could even smell the difference in a dark room such as this. Mob blood was shed quickly and in panic, and had a hyperoxygenated, rusty reek to it.

Having no essential balms, no poultices to apply, and not sure what the boy's reaction might be if he revealed his identity too soon, Bu Yu could only crouch on the far side of the bars and try to make conversation. It didn't matter if the cell mates overheard; most of them were marked for death, anyway, and the remainder seemed to be beggars and mental defectives bound for internal exile.

Bu Yu was slightly amazed and distressed at the sexual babyishness of his doomed little brother: how he blushed when the faceless old whore in the cell across the corridor sat with her legs spread apart, and how he tried not to hear and smell the toilet sounds and reeks of the homosexuals in the corner of his own cell. This was in sharp contrast to the licentious cynicism of many Red Guards in Bu Yu's day.

Even more distressing was the way he almost swooned like a princess from some dead Beijing opera, and babbled to himself about a certain co-ed, his classmate, a reactionary feminist, no doubt, who was the moon and stars to him. Bu Yu had to get him off that.

"Why are you here?" Bu Yu asked, point-blank. Something about his brother's vacant attitude and the madness of the surroundings precluded any social formulae.

"Perhaps I tried to kill my teacher," he said, shrugging slightly and looking at Bu Yu's feet. "You really are barefoot, aren't you?"

"Why did you do that?" asked Bu Yu. "He must have insulted you deeply and made you lose face."

"Well, yes. But one can't blame him for that, can one?"

Bu Yu couldn't reply. Had the indiscriminate, womanish mercy of Christ metastasized even into the dungeon of the Public Security Bureau? Younger Brother took the lack of response as concurrence, and concurrence as an indication that no further talk was necessary.

Bu Yu mustered his strength and whispered, "Why shouldn't one blame a teacher for taking face from his own student?"

"Oh, didn't I tell you he was a foreigner?" "No. So what? Does that explain something?"

"He's an American foreigner." Xiao Bu tried to focus on the strange visitor to see if that cleared it up. Failing that, he apparently decided that a story, a parable or something, might help.

"Let me tell you about these people's sense of face. Once he described to our class what would happen if a typical American had been struggled in the Ten Years' Chaos. Not only would the American not have collapsed and died of shame as many of our people did, including my own father--though I don't remember that--but he would have set the dunce cap upon his head at a jaunty angle and played the gong in syncopated rhythm while dancing and singing his self-criticisms to the melodies of Jewish Broadway show tunes, like this:

> *I'm a cap-i-tal-ist roa-a-a-ader!*
> *Capitalist, do or die!*
> *A real-life nephew of John Maynard Keynes,*
> *Gimmee three-fourths of that pie!*

Bu Yu felt a brief surge of dread upon hearing this story. Some of the mental defectives began barking gibberish along with Xiao Bu, mercifully covering up his English song before the jailers could hear and single him out as an intellectual.

"The American would be glad to have the audience, see?"

"Yes, well, perhaps you shouldn't sing quite so loud, at least not foreign songs. I'm not so sure that even one of your insane Americans would be glad to have an audience under these circumstances."

"No, you still haven't gotten the point," said Xiao Bu. "Americans consider our traditional fears of face-loss trivial and petulant, because they are complete in themselves, like the big fat ugly chunks of rock they build their temples and public buildings with, see? These circumstances wouldn't bother them. I mean, they'd be uncomfortable and cold, and would whine louder than the most pampered dynastic Chinese aristocrat; but deep down inside of themselves, past the pain, they'd only be amused by this detention cell. I've understood that now for about one week. I think I suspected it before I even tried to kill him."

"Then why--?"

"Because in our literature class he consistently and deliberately failed to hew to the socialist/realist line. He taught mostly bourgeois pornography, full of the Western notions that were responsible for the students taking to the streets as they did recently. The people of this town have always been famous for their complacent mentality. It had been a safe bet that ours, of all the students in China, would not have misbehaved themselves. But then this foreigner got their glands worked up by distributing his nauseating novels, tantalizing and piquing the bad elements among the underclassmen into making an attempt to indulge in some Caucasoid-style hell-raising."

Bu Yu's chest swelled with involuntary pride. Younger Brother had tried not to slaughter, but to assassinate.

But then the boy said, "The other demonstrators were not like me. I tried to introduce a level of political consciousness into the marches--"

Bu Yu heard this and almost lost control of himself. He felt like spanking Xiao Bu, which he'd never once been tempted to do in the old days.

"That's the real reason you're in here, isn't it?" he cried. "I knew it! Nobody cares enough about that fat white clown to detain a party member like you for making an attempt on his life. How could you get involved with those young revisionists? I thought you were trying to work within the party for reform or something. The students are just trying to move things even further in the direction of ruination. What would Mama have said if--"

At the mention of her the tears gushed out, the grime washed from his cheeks, and the two brothers suddenly faced each other. Xiao Bu's eyes widened for one second.

"I knew you'd come."

"So why didn't you wait for my help?"

"I didn't want your help."

"You were just kidding me a second ago, weren't you?" Bu Yu pleaded. "Tell me you were just using your party affiliation to lead your classmates like pigs to the abattoir. You knew their misbehavior would speed thereinstatement of the brighter Red policies on the local level, right?"

Xiao Bu laughed in his face, though not maliciously. He revealed in one sad look that his classmates wouldn't have followed him to a gratis banquet of chicken breasts, that they disrespected him precisely because he was party representative. They openly ridiculed him, shouted him down. Bu Yu was speechless.

"How's Grampa?" asked the boy with a smile.

Bu Yu looked up. "Well as his age would lead you to expect. He wants you to have this money, if you'll promise not to spend it on books, but to bribe the jailers into slipping you a spoonful of oil with your rice husks. I can see each of your ribs, except for the broken ones with swollen tissue massed around them. But I suppose you're going to use that old adage on me about protuberant ribs being the badge of the true revolutionist."

Xiao Bu had another saying in mind. "By his stripes we are healed," he murmured.

Bu Yu was certain that galling sentence had come into Younger Brother's head at the same moment it had come into his. Bu Yu did not know if he was ready, if he would ever be ready, for what was coming next.

"She's alive," said Xiao Bu.

Bu Yu was neither surprised nor unsurprised. The thought of Mama had always crossed their minds at exactly the same times, had doubtlessly been doing so over the past decades, even across the hundreds of li. The mere fact of the physical intactness of someone who'd commandeered such a presence in two young men's minds seemed almost incidental.

At this point Younger Brother slipped into a habit of the older peasants at the village, something from remote antiquity. In troubled times, they filled their conversation with well-being refrains, closing off each breath of speech with one of a limited number of formulae, a kind of incantatory charm. The two boys had picked it up. They'd taken a childish comfort in it at bedtime. Talking like this was a way to drown out the screeches of the jungle animals that scratched at Grampa's door.

"She's down in the bowels of this building, in solitary these twenty years, and everything is well.They've been marching us past her on Sundays so we can jeer as she prays to the Blessed Virgin, yet all is as it should be. She knew me immediately, I think, but for my sake she hasn't shown it. There's nothing to be concerned about. She'll die in here, but I won't be quite so lucky. And everything is as one would wish it to be."

All Bu Yu could say was, "There, there. I know, I know."

The boy was looking at thirty years' confinement, at least, with a probable transfer to Qinghai death camp once this cell had gotten so crowded that the dead were piled too high to admit more living. His already tenuous party connections had forsaken him; and, with a civilly dead brother, a literally dead father and a mother located someplace no legal entity could define, nobody remained to sue for Younger Brother's release. He would languish here indefinitely among the pale lizards and fungus and leering bad elements, unless a bribe could be arranged. But the Bu brothers were both paupers and had no friends but a grandfather in the deep countryside who'd already given them his all.

Even as Bu Yu squatted in a blackened puddle and watched between the bars, his brother's emaciated face became cold and empty. Xiao Bu had finally become Chinese.

Bu Yu now learned what it meant to lose one's heart in the common struggle. He could crouch here and watch his own flesh and blood turning to stone and not be moved. He felt no grief, but only a further consolidation of his resolve; and that was as close to shedding individuality as any Chinaman could come, for he had no self to shed save that wrapped up in his nuclear family' and, to a lesser extent, in the "cooked people" in his life. And who "cooked" did Bu Yu have any more? In losing his brother like this, Bu Yu lost Bu Yu.

All the better to throw his lost self into action. His lungs expanded till they nearly cracked his rib cage--even as he had a premonition regarding the soft fuzz on the nape of his brother's neck, which he used to stroke, coaxing the boy to sleep when the beasts had been loud in the hills at night.

He forgot to say goodbye, but the small pebble on the cell floor named Xiao Bu probably didn't notice anyway.

Bu Yu delivered himself from the yellow grime of theP.S.B. headquarters. He burst past the multiple guards with such conviction that whoever had lent him the razor forgot to ask for its return, and he strode out between speeding buses and trucks into the middle of Red

Flag Square.

He did something now for the first time in his life, something he had always fantasized about in certain other city squares, but had refrained from doing for fear of being disrespectful. Another reason he hadn't performed this action before was that it involved the use of the heel of a shoe, and at his most jubilant times in the past, he'd somehow always been shoeless, just as now.

No matter. He went among the new crowds, requisitioned a good-sized plastic sandal from the lip of the murky reflecting pond and climbed the stone base of the Mao statue. In exultation, by the scarlet light from the sunset behind the mountains, he banged on the miraculously stain-free bronze, expecting a peal of the ringing might of socialism.

He got only a hollow, rubbery thud. They were going to shoot his baby brother in the back of the neck.

Joint Venture

*Just our usual one, with the white stripes painted black and the stars
replaced by the skull and cross-bones.*
Mark Twain's suggestion for a Philippine flag

Midnight Mass has just finished at the cathedral of a certain large
Japanese city. Among the crowd of shriven faithful who empty
with placidity into the street are two American automotive executives,
one skinny and one fat, both tall, both from Michigan. They're in
town pursuing gargantuan joint-venture deals with the Ichinuki Motor
Corporation, and are being seen to by the eldest son of Mr. Ichninuki
himself.

These Americans are on the elbows of their lovely wives, but
not for long. Late as it is, they are expected to spend the next few
hours bonding with their various Japanese counterparts. Nothing
naughty will be done, they assure their wives: just a bit of compulsory
watered-down Suntory whiskey guzzling at a boring but elegant little
bar nearby.

"You understand, dear," the tall one says. "In this country, it's
the only way men can speak frankly with each other. No ladies
allowed, all very sexist, and so on. But it's the culture, and interesting,
right?

And the wives, who have tagged along, clear across the
Pacific, to learn about kimonos and flower arranging, do understand.
Automotive joint venture is a most delicate affair.

A couple of black stretch-limousines wait in the shadows at
the cathedral's side gate. The first contains Mr. Ichinuki the Younger,
who emerges, greets the American automotive executives coolly, and
directs them to the second limo. Then he ushers the wives into the
first, and sends them back to their lovely suites at the Marriott.

After the wives have had the chance to be driven well out of
sight, a liveried chauffeur opens a silent black door, and reveals a
couple of bewildered Filipina virgins, huddled and quaking in the vast
back seat. Before the Americans close in on them, these creatures
crane their perfect necks to get a glimpse of God's house.

Exploited and abused as they are, they've managed to wring
this concession from their boss. Only girls who've been "behaving
themselves" are allowed to come near the cathedral. Being from the
Shinto tradition, their Yakuza slave masters have no concept of

communal worship, and assume that points will be tallied in the heavenly score book if the faithful simply approach the precincts. So they see no reason to allow the Filipinas to enter the hallowed presence.

The fat auto executive climbs in, panting, not necessarily from the exertion. "You ladies surely do smell pretty tonight," he guffaws. "Just like a breath of fresh, clean air." He lays hands on the tinier one, a pubescent child with bright golden eyes. "Honey, I'm god-damned if you're not the spitting image of NBC's Connie Chunk!"

She screams in revulsion, shoves him away, and bolts out the door, pushing past Mr. Ichinuki, the younger, who is waiting on the sidewalk, according to cordial Japanese custom, ready to wave and bow until the honored patrons drive out of sight.

His face inscrutable, he gives a subtle nod to a fleet-footed thug riding shotgun in the limo. This human cheetah chases the golden-eyed girl about half a block, and stops her with a flying tackle. She screams again as her beautiful face scrubs into broken glass and gravel in the gutter.

"Looks like that one's out of commission for the night," says the fatter American automotive man. "I guess we're going to have to double up now." He clears his throat and raises his voice. "I hope this means we get a fifty-percent discount!"

That broad hint is lost on Mr. Ichinuki, the younger, for he's gazing thoughtfully up at the steeple, examining the Roman gallows affixed at the tip of such a prideful pinnacle.

* * * *

"Body of Christ, eh Love?" murmurs a middle-aged Filipina who looks exactly like Imelda Marcos. Not only could she be the real Imelda's twin, but she has mastered the identical hyper-emotional acting style: the cheeks that can flush or blanch at will, the tear ducts seemingly connected to faucets in her pockets. She is none other than Imelda II.

It's the next Sunday at the local Yakuza office, and she's dressed in her best outfit: a vulgar sequined dress, precisely the same shade of pale turquoise which swathes figurines of the Virgin Mary in Catholic churches.

In her pudgy hand, which is spangled with glossy vinyl fingernails and pinchbeck rings, she clutches a wadded-up white rag. She's trying to stuff it between the gorgeous but lacerated lips of the golden-eyed girl who bolted from the Americans in the stretch-limo.

"This is as close as you're getting to communion for a long, long time," murmurs Imelda II in Tagalog. Her upper body is powerfully developed, and she's holding down the girl with one hand while trying to gag her with the other.

The victim has been allowed neither to bathe nor bandage her cuts and contusions. She is barely recognizable under the ground-in gravel and broken glass from the gutter where she was tackled.

In English she moans, through teeth shattered, but clenched nevertheless to fend off the gag, "I'm sorry, Den Mother, I'm sorry! I won't run again! It's just that the old American smelled so bad, like poisonous gas! I couldn't help it, I couldn't breathe!"

The den mother calls her attention to certain soothing sounds which echo down the corridor from a back room. The other white slaves are rehearsing a lovely offertory hymn in four-part harmony plus descant, accompanying themselves on their rickety guitars.

"Your big sisters and brothers sing for you," whispers Imelda II, with the mechanical cadences of someone who's just doing her job. "They've been through this, and I as well, and we survived. You will, also. It's part of the burden of being a grown-up lady. So, don't spoil their song with unhappy sounds from your own throat. Bite this rag. It's better than chewing your tongue off, right? And we wouldn't want to alarm the neighbors."

Even while struggling to insert the wad of greasy fabric, Imelda II theatrically averts her eyes, to spare herself the sight of such pitiful pleading. Soulfully, she gazes out the window at the otherwise nice residential neighborhood in which this mob clubhouse is blatantly located.

It being Sunday notwithstanding, this is a regular business day for such a hard-working organization. Dozens of thugs, in their conspicuous costumes and tattoos, brazenly punch in and out with bags full of drug money and crates of contraband handguns purchased on the mainland from corrupt People's Liberation Army officers.

Some neighborhood housewives are gathered around a laundry pole next door. With open scowls, they survey this scene over the back yard fence, and express their resentment.

"This street is getting very busy lately, isn't it, ladies?" one of them says, and the others all concur.

Meanwhile, their husbands slink off with golf bags bigger than themselves, to the driving range for the week's few minutes of pleasure, heads hidden behind slumped shoulders, fearful eyes averted from those of the invaders.

"Pray now to the Blessed Virgin for forgiveness," intones Imelda II.

"I'd rather pray to God the Father," replies the golden-eyed girl, trying to be brave. "Please, Den Mother, may I?"

"Of course, Love," she says, magnanimously. "And I'll join you."

As they say the Lord's Prayer together in Tagalog, the fleet-footed thug who tackled the girl last week approaches from the opposite corner, his stockinged feet whistling along the quaintly traditional tatami mats. He's a sallow reptilian man, with glazed eyes, like a taxidermist's plastic inserts. Over his head he swings something wet, which whizzes and whirrs and flings off moisture that splats in arcs against the walls: a wet, knotted knee sock. (It hurts more than dismemberment and can even cause internal hemorrhaging, but doesn't bruise the goods.) He closes in on the child very slowly, to add suspense to the horror.

The closer he gets, the wider her golden eyes grow. She starts to shriek and convulse a bit, in anticipation of the mistreatment.

"There, there," smiles Imelda II. "It's not quite as much fun as running down the sidewalk in the cool nighttime like a wild puppy, is it? But it's better than being back in our homeland. Be strong now, and the old man might not have you deported."

Then she turns to the lieutenant and snarls, in fluent Japanese gutter dialect, "Okay, okay, Godzilla. You've made your point. Hurry up and get this Jezebel chastised. It's almost time for mass."

Little General Goes Down on the Fu-Wu-Yuan

I don't worry about not having a good position.
I worry about the means I use to gain position.
Confucius

"This comrade is making his way to the provincial capital to research the merchandising techniques of various regional free-marketeers on behalf of our production team. For the sake of the Motherland's glorious Four Modernizations drive, please give him every consideration you can."

The fat lady sneered down from the metal steps. The train was just pulling out, Bu Yu trotting alongside. She blew her nose on the letter and flipped it down on the concrete at his feet. Though it was a forgery and hardly worth losing an arm for, he dove for it and almost fell under the wheels.

"Here's every consideration I have to give," she said, holding out a short-handled toilet broom.

The train was starting to reach a speed at which Bu Yu would have to leap to get on.

"I'll teach you a new meaning of 'link with the masses' that you never imagined in your so-called Cultural Revolution. You still interested in the ride, little man?"

Bu Yu grabbed the broom by the shitty end, which was all she offered him, and swung on behind. As soon as both of his feet hit the grating, her presence enveloped him. Now he was the official fu-wu-yuan's assistant for this leg of the journey through the hills to Putian.

* * * *

It was from this train--not just this line number, but the very car itself (the vague indentations of Maoist slogans they'd carved into the benches were still visible)--that the locals had thrown his Red Guard brigade when it became apparent that none of them were fluent in this particular mountainside's dialect.

It had been in the midst of the worst Taiwan scare in months. Provoked into rash action by the lies of secret representatives of the local power structure, a group of well-meaning factory workers had pooled their small cash reserves and sent a collective telegram to the Central Committee in Beijing, warning them that a Hungarian-style coup attempt was imminent in the provincial capital. They claimed that a vicious gang of middle school dropouts, who wore counterfeit arm bands and pretended to be legitimate "little generals" as a ploy to disguise their dirty activities, were planning to attack the party headquarters and debilitate the leadership in preparation for a Guomindang counter-attack.

Unintentionally substantiating the claims that they had spies in the area, Radio Taibei had sent out a cleverly-worded message at this time insinuating that such a counter-attack would be far from the realm of impossibility once the regional party organization had been softened up by "valiant, right-minded mainland youth."

The effect of this diabolical broadcast was to discredit Bu Yu's brigade and to defame their actual intentions, which had simply been to obey the Sixteen Key Directives of the Eleventh Plenum of the Eighth Central Committee of the CCP: to purge local leaderships of power-factionists who took the capitalist road.

To nobody's surprise, Beijing ignored both the telegram and the broadcast. Nevertheless, with an efficiency rare among these people, the natives printed several hundred thousand copies of the telegram and distributed them everywhere, even across the breadth of this remote mountain. Everybody became suspicious of groups of more than three young people who spoke with strange accents. Bu Yu and his comrades were not the only ones to be thrown from moving trains.

They had just come from the notorious 8-17 incident in Putian: open combat in the streets, their Molotov cocktails, slingshots and cooked stones up against the Third Middle School's Soviet-built Kalashnikov AK-47 assault weapons. Liberated from a PLA surplus dump, rusty, many lacking magazines, firing pins, etc., the guns had been brandished for intimidation purposes mostly; but some spewed occasional automatic fire, distributing fatalities with reasonable fairness between each faction. Bu Yu had seen comrades' heads split wide open at the bone seams, and many of the girls were carried off bleeding.

The survivors had just been riding this train to get home so they could bind their wounds and regroup in time for the scheduled storming of the party headquarters. They had no intention of aiding any counterrevolutionary strike from the fascists' island stronghold. They huddled in an unoccupied corner of the hard sleeper section, trying to conceal their own flowing blood, trying not to say anything, somehow managing to keep their teenaged hearts from bursting out in conspicuous weeping.

But it wasn't until they were deposited at two o'clock in the morning in this wilderness that panic had threatened to overtake the ranks of the little army. Not only the darkness and the horrible ghosts it might conceal, but the countryside itself terrified them: snakes and tigers and water buffaloes with naked rice urchins fastened to their humps like blood-lice; the very open spaces themselves, rivers, hills, sky. The moon blinded their bruised eyes, unencumbered by her customary shroud of city soot.

"We will undergo our own little long march," proclaimed Commander Yue, who feared nature somewhat less than the others because she'd been an early victim of the first experimental rustication programs. Three years running, she had heroically filled more than her share of the farm labor quota, on behalf of some lesser girls whose health would've broken under the strain.

"We should learn from the heroes of 1934, who embarked from these very hills upon a march of 25,000 li," said Commander Yue.

But, in spite of the inspirational parts of Liberation mythology, the rank and file of Bu Yu's brigade had been unable at that moment to forget the sanguinary losses the Chairman had suffered at the hands of warlike Mantzu tribesmen and Xifan nomads in the wastes of Qinghai. China was a whole world, and the world had many lightless folds in its flesh, where diseased organisms shielded themselves from the light of Marxist-Leninist-Mao Zedong Thought. For all their talk of learning from the peasants, the young urbanites still feared the unknowable, gibberish-speaking, black-skinned tillers of the dirt. This was a Proletarian Cultural Revolution, wasn't it? The peasant revolution was yet to come--or, wait, hadn't it already taken place? None of the teens could think straight enough to sort it out. They kept hearing coughs and spitting out there in the inky blackness.

The farmers in these parts used the catamenia of virgin urbling girls as the active ingredient in a special mulch that made their lichees and longans and loquats extra sweet. Everybody knew that was how they managed to achieve the status of model commune harvest after harvest.

To make things worse, the provincial Party Secretary, in a desperate attempt to salvage his credibility and cling to his crypto-monarchist throne, had declared an anti-crime campaign, which conveniently served as an excuse to rid the capital of Red Guard factions more loyal to Mao Zedong Thought than to himself. But the literal-minded militiamen had run many members of the hooligan and criminal classes up into the jungle with the threat of a bullet in the back of the neck, followed by a breakable bayonet between the ribs.

If warlock splinter-Daoist peasants didn't get the stranded youngsters, cutthroats from town would.

The girls had already said goodbye to their maidenheads. They began to squeal and swoon among the stinkweeds like princesses in some dynastic opera. And it was only the feel of the girls' bleeding arms on their shoulders that kept the boys from bolting away from the rail lines and into the open-pit grave of the underbrush, or just collapsing and dying right there of exposure, starvation and horror.

And so their famous Little Long March along the tracks began.

They hid in the jungle outside each village until well past dark, marching only at night. It took twenty days to complete a journey of less than 150 li. Most of their families had given them up for dead. In those chaotic times there was every reason to suspect death and few ways to confirm it.

Train security had taken their knives away, so they had to use bare teeth to get at the pith of the wild sugar cane that grew in sporadic patches near the rails. When their teeth began to ache from the strain and excessive sweetness, the braver brigade members tried to live off strange nuts and berries which they gathered and gagged down as original botanical field research, like Mao searching for smokes along the route of the first Long March. Everybody else tried and failed to catch frogs, which began to look succulent and ample enough to deserve their traditional nickname of "field-chicken." They all upped their caloric intake with garbage thrown from the trains, trying inside their minds not to draw the obvious parallels between themselves and their dessert.

Several months later, when Chairman Mao encouraged the teenagers of China to emulate the early People's Liberation Army with their own little ordeals, Bu Yu's brigade was way ahead of everybody. Toughened and inspired by that midnight march, they had already instituted their Spartan Youth League, a physical culture and health reform program. They had fasts, winter swims, shirtless sojourns in the sleet of autumn. Sometimes they ate only lard and uncooked mung beans to put calluses in their bowels. All within the gates of the city. Tough as they were, the countryside had cowed them.

Younger Brother sometimes joined in, all the while reminding everybody of the philosophy behind their actions. "This is not just a test of individual prowess," he'd squeak in his sparrow voice as Mother dragged him home to do his lessons. Later she would use shocking words to curse Bu Yu for the damage to Younger Brother's health.

* * * *

But now Bu Yu could see that the physical training of his youth, to stand him in good stead, should not have consisted of such constitutional privations. He should have spent the time soaking his head in vats of fermented cabbage, stuffing his nose with cigarette ashes, eating terrible sugary things from plastic bags, and withstanding the foul breath and fouler language of a hag in a blue China Rail uniform. Such disciplines would have prepared his stomach for this train ride today.

He was expected to perform the woman's work of cleaning the car--and it seemed likely that this was the first time anybody had considered doing it since the start of the fat lady's tenure as fu-wu-yuan. But, unfortunately, not much custodial work could be done.

The benches, the tea tables between the benches, the aisles, the windowsills, the baggage racks, even the toilet floor, every solid surface, in fact, was covered with at least one layer of immobilized human flesh, maybe 300 reminders that the population of this province had more than doubled since the last time Bu Yu had gone near a train. Even if he'd been able to reach the windows, he'd not have been able to wash them, for they were flung open so people and their luggage and their livestock could be hung outside. If nobody had lost a head or a limb on a utility pole on this trip so far it was a miracle--proof of the existence of the myriad gods these people still believed in and bribed with joss sticks and tempted by placing themselves in idiotic situations like these.

If Younger Brother were to rise from the grave and materialize at this point, he would probably narrow his eyes and ask, "How much less idiotic was it for a mob of adolescents to engage the Party Secretary's machine-gun-toting personal guard with heated stones and ten-centimeter toy daggers?"

But correct ideology neutralizes idiocy. And where was the ideology, correct or incorrect, on this train? There was no hint of political action or debate among the passengers, though Bu Yu saw countless possibilities.

Occasionally a rich peasant bulldozed through on his way to the soft-sleeper compartments, extending invitations to the select few to briefly enjoy a privilege formerly reserved for high cadres and foreign dignitaries--living proof, with fragrant, pink fingernails, that positively everything was for sale now. And nobody stopped him for quotationizing or rose up and slashed his black throat. When the passengers' mouths weren't stuffed with cheap cigarettes or hand-rolled hemp cigars, they emitted sinewy wads of phlegm, a characteristic habit of these farm people. Their ideology formed puddles.

Nobody was inclined or even able to move around much. The situation was exacerbated by eight hoodlums who had occupied the toilet floor for the sake of a few centimeters' extra leg room. Their noses were probably insensate from having been broken repeatedly in street brawls.

Many people had chosen to maintain a semi-asphyxiated inertia. Rather than bestir themselves they urinated down their trouser legs and, by capillary action, up the trouser legs of their neighbors. Here was concrete proof of the feudal maxim: slothful people piss often.

Motion was communicated indirectly to their lethargic bodies by the car as it feebly negotiated the many switchbacks that snaked through this rugged coastal range, and by the frequent unannounced stops to allow the engineer to steal sugar cane from the railside communes.

"These stalks were accidently broken off by the people's cow-catcher," the engineer would cry out to the peasants as they ran to catch the escaping train. "Truck and bus drivers get to eat their road kill, so why shouldn't I? You should teach your cane to stay out of the way, just as your roadside colleagues teach their pigs and chickens."

At one point the baggage rack collapsed under the weight of about twenty people. It smashed into the head of a mother publicly suckling a three-or four-year-old boy according to the barbaric custom of this mountainside. The impact opened up her scalp and knocked her cold.

The boy's screams were so loud that eventually even these bumpkins decided to move their arms and legs. At the next sugar cane stop they passed the pair through an open window to some harvesters who were gathering up a fighting force to protect their crop from the railway personnel. The peasants were so puzzled by the gift that they just formed their arms into a hammock and received it. They hardly had time to open their mouths before the train got rolling again.

The fu-wu-yuan, representative of officialdom, leaned over the windowsill, mostly to help a fart gain passage between her mammoth buttocks. But, since her mouth was hanging out the window anyway, she bellowed, "My first-aid kit's been pinched by a ticketless stowaway in here! Find that woman a 'barefoot doctor!'"

They just stared at her. Everybody knew that the peasants no longer enjoyed the services of even those amateurs. They'd all been allowed to return to the cities to become entrepreneurs among the proletariat.

The seat vacated by the mother and child was bloody, but the most powerful passengers fought their ways into it by turns. They brushed off wood splinters and settled themselves down, seeming quite mollified with their new position in life. Bu Yu thought he saw a few minor knife wounds inflicted here and there as the people divided up the contents of the young mother's bag.

Such were the effects of Deng Xiaoping's craven revisionism on the socialist spirit of Bu Yu's homeland.

He stood all night except for extended recesses in the "office" of the fu-wu-yuan. She dragged him there sometimes, breathing hard in his face and threatening to have the people throw him off "again." (How did she know about the first time?) She forced him to get down and kowtow to her.

"I'm Empress Wu Zetian. I'm a railroad cadre." She moaned it over and over again. "Wu Zetian...railroad cadre..."

The cubbyhole was so cramped that his face knocked, not against the mass of compressed cigarette butts that constituted the floor, but against her jellied blue-twill lap, which trembled with-- what? The vibrations of the tracks, or some aberrant passion? He realized with a cold sensation that there were indentations in the floor, rubbed by the knees of a succession of unticketed "assistants" before him. This was a habit of hers. Had each of them come equipped with an ersatz letter of recommendation?

But then the rank mountains spread their thighs and opened out into the gentle terraced hills that announced the flood plain of Putian, where Bu Yu had a good comrade to look up. He got up from his knees, dropped his toilet broom, and lost himself in dreams among the rice paddies as the sun came up. He stared between bodies out a thin slice of window, even as the empress threatened and screamed, then actually did have him thrown out on the outskirts of Putian.

She correctly assumed that the country people would be too

meek or stuporous to help her; but even the vacationing college students refused.

"Why should we do your job?"

"Because it is your civic and moral duty to aid a public servant in time of need!" she screeched, and they laughed at her.

By the time the guards finally came around and confiscated his shoes ("He stole them right off me!" she shrieked, displaying hooves twice too large for Bu Yu's poor slip-ons), the students had pressed a cool green bottle of Snowflake beer into his hands, plus two loose-skinned Mandarin oranges which had been donated by a family of farmers.

"Good luck, Big Brother!" they cried after him as he rolled and bounced down the embankment, protecting the beer with his arms, taking the blows with his face. "Walk carefully, Uncle!"

The fu-wu-yuan lorded it over him from the door of the receding train, triumphantly and mistakenly assuming that she had caused him to abandon his "research trip" to the capital.

He would make the rest of the journey by some means other than China Rail, after he had linked up with formidable Hong Ma Han, the Red Horseman.

Nuisance Call

Take away the prostitutes from human affairs, and you'll throw everything into a chaos of lusts.
Saint Augustine, De Ordine ii, 4

Chica wondered why she'd never gotten around to painting her vast elbow man--aside from the prohibitive cost of the several gallons of cirrhosis-yellow pigment it would take. But it was never too late, as long as Biffy's face hadn't relaxed to the point of sliding off his skull altogether.

Maybe she could arrange for him to sit for a formal portrait. What a nice idea!

* * * *

Biff was too irritated to be astonished when he found himself making gestures in the direction of the phone several seconds before it began to ring. The only thing that persuaded him to get vertical at all, it being three a.m., was that his sleeping wife must never, under any circumstances, be exposed to the person who was, without a doubt, on the other end of the line.

* * * *

Only three rings. Yes, the old Bifferoonie was still cultivating that fetch-it boy style--if "cultivate" was the word. It had probably started out as an act, or sheepish overcompensation for taking up so much of other people's space. But what a wimp it finally turned him into. Biffy was a moved and a shook. Shook right out of the marriage bed.

Chica remembered when she used to get screwed, and the more or less precise moment when she'd decided to start doing the same unto others instead of letting it be done unto her. She'd been inspired by watching the old sperm whale in those days, Mr. Premature Personality Disintegration himself, in the flower of his young manhood. Biffy was already so charbroiled that he could barely lift his feet, one after the other. You could hear him coming down the beach at Galveston during a hurricane alert, for God's sake.

* * * *

Even after twelve years, he had only to hear the voice. The caller didn't need to identify herself to achieve the desired effect.

This soul-chewer was always going to turn up, for as long as they both should live, during those times when his moral immune system was in a weakened condition. Chica would crop up simultaneously with thoughts of mortality, regardless of the remoteness of the backwater he'd hidden himself in. Whenever he was in a lightless mood, her voice would sound in an electronic hiss only millimeters away from the skin of his brain, summoning him, at three a.m., to join her in yet another bout of antisocial behavior.

She never had the courtesy to inform him of what that behavior might be until it was two-thirds accomplished. So it wasn't surprising to hear her hang up in his ear after supplying a stripped-down skeleton of details, only what he absolutely needed to know.

* * * *

Chatting up sleepy Biffy, listening to him whisper so as not to roust the old ball and chain--this was like a slap in the face with chilled astringent. It was clear to Chica now that she was in the full fervor of a reaction against his sort of laxity. By her own garter straps, as it were, she'd lifted herself up, and turned herself into a--what? Surely something more than just a dope-peddling rim-job queen.

What was she now? If she were male, "a man" would carry many of the connotations she was striving for. "A woman," even at this late date in the movement, was not quite adequate, unfortunately. Just put it this way: Chica had turned herself into an adult, a grownup, an individuated somebody-or-other. And a painter of some skill: the Paintrix.

* * * *

The earth had bumbled a dozen times around the sun since Biff's last bout of swinishness, before he'd met his wife and settled down--precipitated was a better term, like 350 pounds of coarse sediment. Roughly four-thirteenths of his life had drained off since he'd taken leave of the dominatrix who just jangled him out of bed.

Back when he ran with her, the gay community gazettes in major population centers had just been starting to mutter about a strange, seemingly communicable form of cancer appearing on the soles of the feet of the readership. But nobody had thought to warn the heteros who just liked snickering over the personal ads. And right about now, a mini-lifetime later, a certain unpleasant physical disorder--a whole potential syndrome of them, in fact--should be coming into a certain faithful husband's life, if it were coming at all. The purple splotches were about due.

Like a good middle-ager, he should be getting his gout pills and eating them three a day. But he was afraid that the family doctor, perhaps leery of all convicted felons (even one so manifestly unpopular), might sneak an HIV test into the routine blood workup; and Biff was the kind of guy who would rather not know. So he stayed away from the clinic and failed to get his Xyloprim replenished.

* * * *

Was he still worried about his dick falling off, or whatever?

Chica and Biffy had a mutual acquaintance from the old days, a magnificent cock queen, who'd gotten an ambiguous lab result and had to wait six months for the follow-up that would uphold or commute the death sentence. This guy's face had grown wrinkles in that half year, and he was a brave man. The old Bifferoonie would've fretted himself deep into the grave by that time, even without the virus' help, and he'd have gotten religion in the meanwhile and been a big pain in the butt about the whole deal.

Blame would be assigned, guilt apportioned-a blood test was not a good idea in Biffy's sick enough case.

* * * *

Rather than getting examined and putting this implausible fear behind him, Biff had called in sick a week ago, and sat all day in an excessively hot bathtub, trying to purge his person of former misdeeds through hypothermia. Excavating deep into the moldiest closets of his memory, he'd worked out a to-the-hour timetable of when he might last have been exposed. He'd systematically placed square in his consciousness the prospect of death--his own deserved and his wife's undeserved; his every previous notion and bit of behavior rendered retroactively meaningless; all his coldest suspicions about the grim nature of things grounded firmly, once and for all.

He was, he feared, something beyond a borderline solipsist. And that meant his croaking would be the equivalent of the end of the universe, including all the seemingly death-resistant things--such as his love for his wife--that had come into existence before a certain very late, and extremely atypical, morning in Oklahoma City, when he'd been so flabbergasted by his own luck that he neglected to dress Thumbelina in her slicker.

Meanwhile his gouty kidneys languished for want of medication, and plumped with deposits of razor-edged golden gravel that conglomerated into serrated boulders that avalanched, in turn, through his innards and cannoned out the end of his member, until not only peeing, but something so psychologically significant as orgasms felt different now, as they squirted past the scar tissue ever heaping in his urinary meatus. Soon Thumbelina's craw would be obstructed as badly as if she had contracted one of the more venerable forms of social disease for the eighth time and needed scooping out.

Part of Biff couldn't imagine his own non-being. The trouble was that part of him could, and did, several times an hour lately, in each dark, disordered detail. However, there was yet a third part of Biff (the part named Thumbelina), which considered death and universal dissolution a fair price to pay for that one unprotected Oklahoma morning.

* * * *

Yes, Biffy all scrubbed and barbered, his ping-pong table-sized face wearing the pensive expression of a goon no longer young. Biffy, posing to be painted by the Pintrix. It was definitely a nice idea.

Until this moment, she'd never known just how much of an artist she was. She was a maker of images to the very core of her imagination. She had to picture her former elbow man on canvas, pack him between the four edges of a Sears Roebuck frame, before the sheer enormousness of his anomaly hit her. For the first time, and more than a decade too late, Chica understood what should have been obvious all along, plain as a tertiary syphilis chancre exploding on the tip of your nose: Biffy had not been the ideal choice for the coveted position of elbow man.

* * * *

She was a bad memory from the late stages of his brief criminal career, the sinsemilla-hazy years, when the fourth decade of his ever-dwindling existence had started stalking him through the underbrush like a saggy and bloodshot puma. Possessing little else then but the uncanny ability to drive several days on end non-stop with neither a Dexamil nor a wink of the eye, he'd chauffeured her through the desert in an old death trap which a jelly-bellied client of hers had invited them to steal and send over a cliff for insurance purposes: naked interstate sprints with the top cranked down, Chica getting browner and blonder by the mile like a degenerating photo negative. This was before the ozone got officially depleted, but redheaded Biff had still blistered. Carcinomas were about due.

Biff had always been inclined to subscribe to the Leninist view of the happy hooker as a fantasy of the declining bourgeoisie. Prostitutes were just a class of oppressed workers like any other, needing reeducation. But Chica gave the lie to that wholesome conceit each time she told him to stop outside any old high-rise condo in a strange town, and she disappeared into the elevator and came back out forty-five minutes later with a couple hundred dollars cash and a beaming grin of professional pride in herself. She never was disheveled on exit, though sometimes her curls did appear damp, and were redolent of the gentlemanly brands of hair conditioner that Biff could never afford.

* * * *

After jettisoning her pimp, as so many of her sisters in the profession did during that heady era, Chica decided to hit the highway. Just to keep the mega-oaf around as a (barely) breathing reminder of the dire pitfalls of emotional, physical and financial slughood, she cleaned him up and pressed him into service as her elbow man.

Bachelor Biffy needed neither weapons nor phony martial artistry to chaperon her in the Ramada Inns of the sedate, low-competition towns they trolled--Boise, Ogden, Phoenix, El Paso, Oklahoma City, and so on. His surreal bulk was more than adequate, especially accompanied by his everyday facial expression, which murmured, "Would you give me a break? I would seriously advise you to do so."

His job was to loom and brood and burp outside the room where she had a "date." Staring down hotel security with that unsocialized mug of his, he was supposed to knock more frequently than the agreed-upon thirty or sixty minutes, in an effort to bleed timorous johns.

In the elevator on the way up she was always forced to just about splinter his yard-long shinbone with kicks, regular field goal attempts, and other subtle sorts of signals, to let him know which johns could be intimidated by the thump of his gorilla knuckle on the door, and which were absolutely not to be fucked with, except in the literal sense, by her, unassisted, in straightforward business transactions terminated efficiently and calmly as possible. There were more of those scary types each year that American history dragged on; and to Chica, whose ass was literally on the line, the difference was always immediately apparent. But Biffy saw them all the same: just the tops of the heads of guys uniformly lucky to get into the boss' dainty drawers.

Then, unable to leave well enough alone, like a couple of dick-faced morons, they widened their professional horizons. Chica had no idea what kind of hell they were eventually going to get themselves into.

* * * *

Even in tranquil recollection he couldn't nail down the precise epoch when the two of them had branched out businesswise, and they'd begun stopping at times other than when they were absolutely broke, and the tall condos no longer seemed randomly selected, and the stacks of cash she extracted began to get unreasonably tall themselves, and her look of pride de-intensified and became a matter of sheer business rather than performance art. It was only after they'd gone all the way from Dumbass to Wacko, so to speak, that she troubled to inform him of the illicit nature of what, besides her ass, he was suddenly helping to transport across state lines.

* * * *

The other business was fairly homespun in those innocent days, just before the market boomed and heads of state took over, and the regional distributors were able to equip themselves with Lear jets and G-3's. Unarmed small-timers with bad cars and marginal attitudes could make themselves useful back then, especially in the remote Rockies and the deserts of the Southwest, where the towns of any significance whose citizenry knew how to have a good time were few and far between, where even the pimps had names like "Road

Runner." This was before a certain form of contraband got all concentrated, compact, cheap, easy to administer, and vicious, and seeped down into the hands of the Great Unwashed. It was still being passed off as an idle pursuit, a mere affectation of the leisured-or at least middle class, who had access to support groups and aversion therapy and other weaning methods when it came time to dry out and rejoin society. On the entrepreneurial end of things, guilt was minimal and death remained the exceptional occurrence.

Things were literally down-to-earth. She only had to put Biffy on one airplane, and was forced to fuss and linger with him at the security checkpoint, holding his hand and listening to his last will and testament--fortunately short, for he owned nothing. She'd dressed him in a raincoat that balmy Arizona day, weighed down with (he was surprised six months later to be told, having asked no questions at the time, as usual) several hundred thousand dog-eared and sweat-soggy dollars sewn into the lining.

At first, when she still assumed that a normal adult amount of gumption must be hidden somewhere underneath his vaporous stupor, she made the near-fatal mistake of allowing Biffy a little franchise of his own. Predictably enough, he sat on his butt and let the supply degenerate, as organic substances are prone to do (she kept trying to drive that wisdom through his degenerating skull), until it had to be reconstituted, at a loss of thirty to forty percent of its retail value, and she almost got killed at a monthly meet--was compelled to hit her knees and make like a Hoover as she'd never done before or since.

He couldn't be bothered to drop by the junior highs and peddle an occasional oh-zee, so there was always a serious shake problem with his share of the weed as well. Chica could remember excavating among the knee-deep Quarter-Pounder-with-Cheese wrappers in his hovel, and finding Hefty can liners, the kind Jonathan Winters hawked so humorously on television, chock-full of what had been, at one time, ultra-primo hydroponic hothouse red-haired sinsemilla buds. When you touched these bags with the tip of your toe they exploded like overripe seed pods, releasing ten-thousand-dollar clouds of flour-fine powder, with nothing left behind but undergrowths of no-longer supple twigs.

Biffy was virginal of the entrepreneurial spirit, to put it politely. He was a congenital three-toed, matty-haired tree sloth when it came to just about everything in earthly life. He stuck with Chica not for mutual fun and profit, but because, as he moaned into her scoffing face whenever they got drunk on Thunder Chicken, he "saw something worth saving" in her. (She should have known he'd wind up in the Land of Zen, with air-head notions like that.)

Needless to say, the two of them didn't hit their stride, businesswise, until Chica wised up, took over altogether, and quit letting the dumb ox know anything besides what to lift and the general direction to lug it in. Not much of a business partner, to say the least. But he always proved extremely dependable behind the wheel, where his moony mind had only to concentrate on the next hundred yards or so, and was free to wander beyond that in whatever morose direction it chose.

* * * *

Biff flinched as he recalled once getting automotively disoriented in a Tucson barrio, a certain fearless and resourceful woman alighting from the death seat and telling him, as usual, to stay put with the engine running. Chica had gone among a dark knot of youths who were eager to exchange directions for a few "toots" of something which, in those days, in that town, they'd only heard about.

What might, he supposed, be considered the sad thing about all this was that, like so many American women of her generation and socioeconomic class, she claimed to feel the presence of another more legitimate type of artist inside her, itching and bitching to undergo parturition.

"In another life," she said, one time only, when he'd closed his eyes for a moment, "I might have been a painter of people."

Once or twice while she slept and he didn't (the usual case), he sneaked a glimpse at her ultra-secret sketchbooks--miniature and cramped--and saw endless arrays of self-portraits ranged in rows like the walls of a labyrinth she was trying to scratch her way out of. She'd more or less accurately rendered her own tight platinum curls, aquiline nose and steely grey eyes, but had added what he assumed to be unconsciously angry embellishments: grinding incisors and throats knotted with too many blood vessels and flexed sinews.

He'd used what had oozed into his diseased orbits as evidence to convince himself of an obvious falsehood: that a good man's influence, steadfast, normal and true, would eventually soften all the wrenched tendons and yanked-back eyelids and lips, to induce a clearer vision, free of expressionistic distortions. Only now, a huge chunk of life too late, did Biff understand that he'd examined her sketchbooks through eyes sick with love.

Long-term death and disintegration, one way or another: that's what Chica brought. He'd been hoping all this time that her species of soul cannibal only fed on bachelors in their late twenties. But now, a husband in his very late thirties, he knew he hadn't shaken her yet, and probably never would. They were doomed to bump up against each other whenever any birthday approached that ended in that most vain and vexatious digit: zero.

Of course he succumbed. It was like relaxing everything, including the autonomic functions of his body. He deliberately took a deep breath, stepped into his shoes, and delivered himself up to the chaos that hung, anyway, over this imitation of a home and job, this fleeting hiatus of ersatz normalcy, the abyss on either side. Opening the front door was like abandoning his wife on a ridge between jagged sandstone cliffs in a red desert.

In no time a certain boxy family station wagon was lurching into the first of an interminable series of expressway tunnels. It vanished into blackness thick as the fur on a Labrador retriever that fetches anything thrown out in front of its face, heedless of peril to the teeth and tongue. He'd been given the address of a barber who opened early.

There were several painful pit-stops along the way, as daffodil-colored gravel accumulated in a special cup, which his wife had magnetized to the dash for that purpose. The little stones needed analyzing.

Keepsakes

It was a regular Tower of Babel in the crypt chapel. A single language, English, echoed among the jelly doughnuts and seaweed sembei, but it was an English thick with Portuguese, Indonesian, Belgian, Uruguayan, Belarussian, Kenyan, Manchurian and Michigan accents, just to name a few. The parishioners were passing a bundle around. "Ms. Edwine's latest acquisition" is what they had decided to call it.

In the bundle, her sparse black hair still damp from the baptismal font, a beautiful two-month-old was sucking up the attention. She already seemed to recognize her new mother: when Polly Edwine's turn came around to hold her, a certain extra light radiated from under her double eyelids--or did they have single eyelids? Polly could never get that straight.

Then a strange Japanese man appeared. There was a lull in the chaos as everybody eyed him. Natives were not exactly welcomed here. This was as much a once-a-week Japan-bashing session as it was a chance to "fellowship" with Christ.

Someone murmured, "What's this? More Yakuza coming to impose on us?" But it seemed unlikely: nobody had heard the grind of another black windowed van pulling up in the gravel outside. And if this new intruder was a purveyor of human flesh, his winding among the pews lacked the requisite un-Japanese swagger.

He was bent forward at the waist and slightly trembling. When forced to cross anybody's line of sight--not just the mobsters', but even the women's and children's--he bowed even more deeply, held out his hand, and limply karate-chopped the air. It was a gesture of intense, but not necessarily sincere humility, which seemed to say, "Forgive me. I know the light particles bouncing off whatever you're glancing at are infinitely more significant than my miserable person. But contingencies have made it necessary for me to interrupt their flow into your eyeballs for the briefest of instants. Here, let me use the palm of my hand to effect the breach in the gentlest manner. Then I will slip the rest of myself through as unobtrusively as possible."

"Pretty lame genuflection," whispered somebody's adolescent child, in Hiroshima on vacation.

He seemed to be making a beeline for Polly's pew; and it wasn't until he was about three feet away that his eyes became recognizable through the incense smoke and crypt-gloom. (The rest of his face was covered by one of those surgeon's masks affected by urban Orientals with colds or halitosis, real or imagined.) Since her husband's much-bruited "illness," this little man had been following Polly around. She had noticed him most recently loitering outside the prefectural child guidance office after her latest screaming bout with senile adoption officials.

"Mr. Fukuoka has come for his baptismal instruction, and he's a bit early, I should think," said Father Gaudi to nobody in particular, with an uncharacteristic lack of warmth. Oddly, the priest seemed to be maintaining several outstretched arms' length between himself and his masked catechumen.

The festivities resumed. It was a good thing, too, for the new Edwine had been starting to fuss in all the inactivity.

"Pardon me for interfering in your religious worship, Madame," Mr. Fukuoka choked out, "but you left an important thing at the family court yesterday, and--"

There was a gleeful outburst near the sedilia. Apparently the baby had said a word or punched somebody in the face.

Polly's new self-appointed man Friday seemed both agitated and relieved at the interruption. Whatever he had to deliver was making him twitch and flush in embarrassment. His whole body was knotted like a little fist. Then somebody passed the gurgling bundle into his arms.

He said, into her face, "A fine Hiroshima maiden, ne?"

Of all the many pairs of arms she'd visited this morning, Mr. Fukuoka's seemed to fit her best. She was one of his own, after all. But there was something anomalous about his reaction. His words were tender, yet his voice was cold. He bounced the child up and down in the universal manner, but he almost seemed to be hefting her, appraising her like a bag of goods.

Then, from under the jelly-smeared receiving blanket, his wristwatch made one of those tiny blips that can somehow penetrate every corner of a room, even one crowded with rowdy, milk-fed occidentals.

"I admire your charity, Madame," he said as he passed the baby on to her next fan. "But it's so different from the Japanese way. It's maybe the strangest of all the things you gaigokujin do." He glanced at the Nigerian acolyte's shiny white surplice. Under their lids, Mr. Fukuoka's eyes yearned for some kind of enlightenment. "What I'm wondering is, do you intend to keep her forever?"

Polly's whole body lurched forward in her desire to say

everything that should be said about high-priced in vitro quackery and seven-year waiting lists in the U. S., about staving off the despair of encroaching middle age with participation in a brand-new, entirely separate life, about love and floating affection and twelve thousand other things. But the only words her mouth could spout were, "Thomas Jefferson, Jesus Christ--"

Mr. Fukuoka sighed and nodded his head, visibly disappointed. He'd obviously anticipated a Brotherhood-of-Man speech, but had been hoping for something more concrete, or at least more exotic.

"Well," he said, "at least she'll never be able to curse you for bringing her into the world."

Someone from Michigan, an automotive industry man, bellowed, "Hey, Polly! Can I give your new brat a couple slugs of this Suntory Dry? I hear it's great for the kidneys. They'll bring you top price in the States."

This oaf's wife lost no time punching him in his own kidneys. But Mr. Fukuoka was so intent on emptying his face of any reaction that he didn't see. He gazed down at the flowered baptismal candle tucked under Polly's thigh on the pew, next to the baby's snoring older sister. Of course, he immediately divined its function. No matter how "internationalized" they got, no matter how worldly or wealthy, the Japanese would never lose their facility with the irrational, their intuitive grasp of ritual mystery.

"You'll burn this at her funeral, Edwine-san?"

"And at her first communion. Her wedding also, if she wants."

"But not at her divorces or abortions," guffawed the beery Michigan man, who'd sidled near and was eavesdropping. This time his wife silenced him with a firm downward pressure on the shoulders. He plopped next to Polly with a look of mock contrition on his face.

"Don't pay any attention to him," said Polly, but Mr. Fukuoka didn't hear her. He was holding the new white candle in his hands and murmuring to himself, "A beautiful custom, a strong sense of continuity. One would never have expected this among such--"

He seemed finally able to discharge his errand. He handed over a tiny wooden box with a tortoise and crane engraved on its lid, a slip of hospital data pasted to the back. Then he exited, only about half as apologetically as he'd entered.

Inside the box was something wrapped in pinkish glassine, buried in minuscule white crystals. It looked like an unshelled snail, blackened and stretched to an unlikely length, then coiled around itself several times.

It made the same rounds as the bundle, mystifying everybody. Not until it reached the mutilated hands of one of the indigenous Yakuza was an explanation forthcoming. Someone simultaneously interpreted the sandpapery, emotionless voice from the rear of the crypt.

"It's her umbilical cord, preserved in salt. You save it and cremate it with her, so she can be reassembled in the spirit world. All true Japanese are put to rest in this way--"

"You know how tidy the nips are," blurted the automotive man, before thinking better of it.

"--because, even though our bosses are entitled to take away our fifth fingers, our life-lines are our own, forever."

Eventually the automotive man's more obvious jokes about pico-curies and cannibal Eucharist died down. Somebody found the little wooden box a place on the organ bench where it fit nicely, as though it had been there all morning, tucked among the missalettes.

Within fifteen minutes it and the baptismal candle, the baby's other combustible keepsake, had ceased to be objects of conversation.

The Epoxy-Resin Mao

Sam and Mustapha were sprawling on the bamboo mats among the brittle baby toys, proudly nursing their bruises and wondering if Sam's nuclear family would ever get out of bed, when Dean Rong, in tow of the post graduate party informant, came to the door with an ultimatum from "the leaders," whoever, wherever they were.

"The leaders consider what you have done to be an extremely provocative act," Rong said.

Sam assumed that the trembling old man was referring to the previous night's provocative act. Around midnight, he and Mustapha (minus Sam's wife and baby, who had stayed home bathing because there was hot water) tried to get the thousands of kids to bring down the giant epoxy-resin Mao in Hong Qi Square.

"Go home and go back to bed," an underclassman had said in perfect English, sounding almost bored. "This is none of your business."

The police, always the most efficient and clever arm of this state, had sprayed water all over the place a few hours earlier and everybody was covered with bruises from contact with the perfect sheet of ice. The millions of spit gobs had resembled wads of cotton batting suspended centimeters deep in crystal. But to hear Mustapha tell it now, there had been brawls and mean fascists had kicked him in the pants.

Sam and Mustapha had needed entire bottles of baiju to stay warm. Their empties had bounced off the Great Helmsman's rubbery knees like ping pong balls, shattering somewhere among the crowd, the only bottles to break in any demonstration in the country that night. The response had been disappointing. The students were ten to fifteen years younger than the two foreigners, but were displaying very little Confucian elder brother respect.

"We're not vandals. We're not beatniks. This is not America. We're marching to the mayor's compound to make specific demands concerning local politics which you can know nothing about. Go back to your foreign expert buildings and take your Uighur narcotics. We need no American aid tonight."

"You piece of Tibetan duck shit," snarled Mustapha in Chinese, "do I look American to you?" And he informed them of his true nationality.

"Oh? And exactly where is that?" asked one large northern

type at the front of the crowd. "Can you show us on a map?"

Whenever Mustapha began spitting out his native tongue and snapping his black and white shawl around like a bath towel, it was time to get him away from strangers--not an easy job in this country. Sometimes talking to him soothingly worked, sometimes only Sam's superior weight would do.

Last night Mustapha had allowed himself to be more or less arranged on the handlebars of Sam's black bicycle, and they'd spent the rest of the evening trying not to disrupt the baby's feeding schedule.

And now, this morning, as he faced Dean Rong and the post-graduate party spy in the corridor, questions began to congeal halfheartedly in Sam's head.

How could "the leaders" have responded so quickly to a provocative act performed less than six hours ago? Normally at least two days of political study meetings were necessary for a formal censure of a foreign expert. And why send the chairman of the foreign languages department to scold him? Surely inciting-to-riot rated a visit from at least a minor party official.

"Such a topic would never have been allowed--" Rong was saying.

At this moment Sam wasn't going to try to sort out Rong's strange Alzheimer babble about topics. He only knew that there was a more or less venerable Chinaman standing at his vestibule; and anyone who has skimmed the appendix in the cheapest five-and-dime Chinese phrase book knows that a warm welcome, tea and all, is valued above almost everything else in this country.

But Sam had no way of predicting how Rong would mix with his friend. Mustapha had already condemned him sight-unseen as a pseudo intellectual for having mastered English, French, Japanese, as well as his own native dialect and Pu Tong Hua, but not Arabic. Mustapha might easily call him the sallow residue of a noble race before the jasmine blooms had sunk to the bottom of the single university-issue porcelain teacup the baby hadn't yet smashed.

Mustapha loved Sam with a broken-hearted passion, precisely because his people had vowed to slaughter Sam's people one by one if necessary. (Until they'd met, Sam had never really thought of himself as having "people" beyond Polly and the baby.) Mustapha brought to Sam alone his waking nightmare/memories, for all his foreign classmates at the medical university across town had their own third-world horror stories and couldn't bear to hear more--Mibi, the

Ugandan pharmacology major, for example, from whose lower torso entire sirloins had been carefully sliced

That left Sam to hear Mustapha's recitals over and over again: mother and brothers, entire village rocketed straight up into the sky before his nine year-old eyes; passportless sojourns in nations that officially welcomed his kind but treated them like vermin; foolishly distinguishing himself in the makeshift middle school instead of slouching and pimping in the alleys with his refugee cousins, and so, winding up in this filthy hell, studying gynecology on the soft Chinese currency that was extended to his people in the same supercilious spirit that Mormon aid is extended to Tongans; six years of assembly-line abortions, twenty or thirty a day, on suburbanite Chinese women who'd been deflowered too early in life, their vulvas deformed by forced entries; and, as though for variety's sake, the occasional hush-hush sex change operations on cadres' hysterical sodomite sons to forestall threatened Hong Kong escape attempts.

Sam and Mustapha had met on the night Reagan bombed the baby hospital in Tripoli, over a game of eight-ball in the art deco Renmin Hotel. Sam had refused to serve as representative of the American people at an afternoon disturbance outside the U.S. Consulate. (Afternoons were his turn to take care of the baby--he preferred afternoons because her bowels tended to move for Mommy in the mornings.) And so Mustapha had followed him out onto the street and offered to retroactively abort him with a pitiful Shanghai-brand scalpel.

Sam had laid the pretty little Philistine down on the cobbles and sat on him in a reverse David and Goliath scene, and was preparing to scream the customary disclaimers of Reaganite sympathies down into his face, when they'd both looked up and noticed the crowd of nearly a thousand that had gathered in less than thirty seconds. The natives were staring as with a single pair of slanted eyes at two individuals of the same species of sick, hairy, big-nosed zoo animal. And solidarity had instinctively risen in two alien breasts, made them pals, transformed Sam into the full-time manager of Mustapha's homicidal raptures.

In China, gossip is the main product of the workers and their state, the object and result of whatever diligence they display. Nosiness is the party's low-budget K.G.B. and F.B.I. rolled into one. Even a nationally venerated scholar like Dean Rong could be relied upon to care about the behavior of a desert neurotic two generations his junior--unless he had his own neurotic behavior to indulge in. In

Rong's case, this morning, it was one of his own compulsive spiels that made him fail to notice Mustapha's scoffing presence on the other side of the door.

"We are colleagues and good friends," Rong was saying. "You know I suffered a lot in the ten years' chaos. They made big-character posters about me, placed me under house arrest and burned all my poems. They made me write self-criticisms for one year. You are a good man, and I am sure you will understand that you place me again in a difficult situation. I will be criticized severely for not keeping watch over my foreigners."

He glanced and trembled at the party suck who had obviously dragged him here, and he continued. "I give you my solemn word as a fellow scholar and teacher that there will be no persecutions. I've always dealt honestly with you in all our work together, and--"

Mustapha, who had been eavesdropping, shouted from within the apartment, "Tell him he must fuck his mother! In Chinese, cáo ni de ma! Or, wait, is it câo, employing the falling-rising tone? Sammy, where is your Hasner's?"

Sam turned away from Rong, who seemed to be thinking what it would be like to carry out the disembodied request. "Come on, Moosie," Sam said, as quietly as possible. "I'm sure fuck your mother's going to be in Hasner's."

"Sammy, is it proper for you, as a father, to say such dirty things in front of a child?"

The baby, awake now, began trying out the Mandarin fuck-word for herself. After making sure Rong had heard the baby's tiny guttural câo's echoing from the sleeping alcove (she seemed to prefer the falling-rising tone), Sam said, "Forgive me, but I must attend to the child." He shut the door in the leaders' mysterious envoys' puzzled faces--but not before Rong could shout out "--and so I must ask you to give me those examination papers right now, this instant!"

Examination? What examination? Oh yeah, two weeks ago already. Sam had not bothered to glance at them. Now the topic came back to him, along with the string of loaded questions with which he'd filled the glaring, primitive slate chalkboard. The retroactively forbidden exam topic:

Write on the new student democracy movement and its potential impact on your motherland's sagging modernization drive. Take into consideration the following questions:

1. Were big-character posters the workers' last means of self expression?

2. Should democracy be the Fifth Modernization, as certain of our undergraduate comrades who now rot in solitary confinement have suggested?

3. Is that "factory worker" they arrested last night really an itinerant Taiwanese spy with no visible means of support? Is he really intent upon corrupting China's golden youth? Or is he just some poor stooge they pulled at random off the street? Why was his face all puffy and caked with make-up on TV last night? Do you figure your fat leaders tortured him a smidge before he signed that confession?

You may use neither your Hasner's nor any other sources. Write for exactly two hours. At the end of that time, when I say "stop," put down your pencils immediately or flunk. Eyes on your own paper. No crib sheets. No leaving for the toilet. No talking.

It had seemed like a pretty good exam topic at the time. This was supposed to be a course in modern British and American novels, and Sam figured there might be a modern American novel in it somewhere.

Mostly out of curiosity, just to see if it would actually be possible to locate the papers, Sam began to poke among the refuse that cluttered the apartment. He now realized that he hadn't only forgotten about the exam; he'd also forgotten the students' names. Their maddeningly similar names, once so diligently memorized, had passed into oblivion.

He did seem to recall that one boy was nicknamed Trigger. Somehow that was a name Sam couldn't get out of his mind. He wondered if it was in honor of Roy Roger's famous horse, carrying the obvious sexual connotations. There were even more obvious Chinese sexual connotations: pao ma meant riding the horse and also jacking off. Or, perhaps it signified hair trigger, in the sense of premature ejaculation (zao xie in the local street dialect), a dysfunction legendary among the local intelligentsia. In any case, Sam knew he had a Trigger in the class, and his conscious mind no longer had an individual to associate with the name--but his unconscious mind kept sending up insistent, blurry images of an oval face.

Sam had started a model teacher. San Mu Lao Shi, the walking encyclopedia, the post-graduates had called him, and invited him to the reading room to talk. The first semester everybody, Sam as well as the students, had done beautifully on Orwell's 1984. Brave, dangerous things had been said out loud, right in class: a non-revisionist history of the party is impossible to get in China, but, in Hong Kong and America, books as true as Emmanuel Goldstein's are openly distributed; the insidious processes of Newspeak can be recognized in Mao's attempts to "de feudalize" Chinese characters, etc.

Sometimes Sam would get nervous and make discreet warning nods in the direction of the party informant (his head always down, seeing nothing, hearing everything, taking copious notes in the back of the grimy classroom); but the students would laugh and loudly proclaim with one voice, "In China, animals and English students are free!"

In the halls, in the dorms, in the nightmarish restrooms,signs suddenly appeared in English, Chinese, Japanese, even Russian:

WAR IS PEACE
FREEDOM IS SLAVERY
IGNORANCE IS STRENGTH

Then one day the pregnant pinto cat in the cafeteria was no longer pregnant, but no kittens were in sight--just four particularly smug and plump rats lounging in a melted patch of earth out back, an omen.

The students' persuasive essays began to de-politicize and sink to innocuous topics like child-rearing, and to be accepted for publication by the op-ed folks at China Daily, where they'd formerly been rejected with indignation.

Then the class switched, as the syllabus had given ample warning it would, from twentieth-century dystopias to contemporary novels in verse (a bibliographically manageable area of study, Sam assured them). Their pirated offsets of the decadent bourgeois Pale Fire turned out blurry, and the class lost its aim, flopped. No voices but Sam's drone were heard any longer. The party suck (Trigger?) felt the time ripe to move closer to the front of the class.

But the shreds of the 1984 signs still flapped from some of the walls; and it had been, Sam now recalled, mainly to win back the affection of his students that he'd resorted to the pedagogical hooliganism of that exam topic which was causing Rong to twitch so miserably among the barrels of barely preserved cabbages in the black passageway.

"What do you suppose they'll do?" Sam heard himself asking nobody in particular, in a slightly wavering voice. Mustapha held his arms high in the air and said, "Foreign expert expelled from the

People's Republic. Interviews on Voice of America. Book contracts. Hope to stinking Jesus the reactionary pigs will send you home." Then he added, gleefully, "The leaders are probably just now hearing about what we did--"

"Failed to do," said Sam.

"--last night"

"A relatively minor disturbance," said Sam, trying not to sound nervous.

"No thanks to us." said Mustapha.

"Curricular subversion piled on top of extracurricular provocation," moaned Sam. "I wonder how they'll react. I've never seen the Chinese patience pushed to the limit."

"I have," said Mustapha. "At bicycle wrecks. They always have the traditional Confucian conference, instead of appealing to something so barbaric as the law. And teeth bounce all over the pavement during these conferences."

Polly woke up and rolled over. Sam looked into her eyes. She was the rational half of this marriage, and she looked a bit worried.

Sam had evidently become an academic right down to the walls of his arteries. He barely listened to the alarmist insinuations of his guest because he was too busy worrying about his reputation. He didn't want his good name to become politically tainted in the Middle Kingdom and lose the glory which the otherwise cynical Chinese fatuously attached to the Ph.D. that followed it. He couldn't afford to be dissociated from the resume-swelling projects over which he and Rong had been cackling and salivating in the good, golden pre-democracy days of Sam's tenure this side of the Pacific. In spite of their differences at the moment, Rong and Sam shared an almost infinite capacity for typing, self-aggrandizement, and neglect of the classroom.

Now, if he failed to deliver up the exam papers (and, along with them, in effect, the students themselves), Sam would have to retract and trim back down to a page and a half the hundreds of vitae he'd sent to every continent in the world. There would go any chance of escape from China, and any justification for having schlepped Polly to China in the first place.

Mustapha slid a little closer to Sam on the bamboo mat. With a terrible appetite, he ascended to a new plateau of communion. He expressed dark, paranoid thoughts.

"The leaders here are famous, even in China, for Maoist extremism," said Mustapha. "This city was the last bastion of the

Cultural Revolution. If you don't believe this, ask the old man." He twitched his squatty body in mockery of Rong. Laughter almost adulterated his strange passion for an instant.

"Even now," said Mustapha, "during anti-crime campaigns, when most places save their bullets for murderers and rapists and embezzlers of over five figures, here they liquidate boys for saying lascivious things to girls. And what about your predecessor, Sammy? The party line is that he gradually poisoned himself to death with rice spirits in this flat, perhaps on this very mat. But have you ever asked yourself why they didn't just dismiss him from work and send him back to America for his death?"

Polly sat up and said, "In socialist countries they have no apparatus for firing people."

"Did you know he was distributing photocopies of letters smuggled from the democracy-and-freedom pupils' cells?" asked Mustapha. "You know, I never saw him touch baijiu, only beer. If he had taken as much baijiu as they say, one match lit in his vicinity would have been enough to cremate him. But I did see his face swell and I saw his character and his mind turning to rice porridge. How convenient that they burn people here, along with their telltale connective tissues and organs."

Mustapha leaned his head back and began to declaim at the concrete ceiling. "Mibi says our leaders caused the pharmacology majors secretly to cook vats of synthetic hallucinogens in the lab in those days--what the Public Security Bureau calls tougaigu dian, electricity for the top of your head."

"Perhaps better rendered skull lightning," said Polly.

"They know how to paint doorknobs and bicycle handlebars with that poison, and it can pass through the flesh of your hand. Just ask your former Minister of Security, G. Gordon Libby, whose fruit company has enslaved countless thousands of peasants in South and Central America."

Mustapha began to elaborate further on the seamy side of American foreign policy, but the baby stopped him with a scornful fart noise from between her boneless gyms. Bored, she eased herself off the bed to play in a pile of toys and papers.

"If you go crazy and die they will try to take the baby away from Polly because she is only a woman."

Polly said, "Never. They have no concept of social services."

Sam wanted to absorb the tiny round girl into his matted chest hair. He forgot about publishing and began to think about perishing.

How could Polly manage with him a pile of ashes? And the Chinese liberating his daughter was out of the question. They tied babies' arms and legs down with garish dish towels, leaving only their genitalia exposed and freezing, and they tormented them by waving battery-operated toys in their faces all day.

"Damn! If I could only find those fucking exams!"

Mustapha put his nightmare on hold and stared at him. Polly stared also.

"You lost the exams? What kind of teacher are you?" cried Mustapha. "What did they say?"

"I didn't get a chance to look at them."

Shocked silence from a man whose village was rocketed to toothpicks when he was nine.

"You lost them in this flat somewhere?" asked Polly.

"I assume so."

"Then we will find them," said Mustapha. He glanced into the sleeping alcove at the eight-month-old supply of ungraded post-graduate themes, a baby of similar age with universal solvent saliva making papier mache from the flimsy pages.

"Maybe we'll find them," said Polly.

"No, we must find them," said Mustapha. "The leaders would never want them made known. Most of the cadres are planning trips to America soon to purchase the Three Bigs, and they don't want their exit visas jeopardized by attention paid to political unrest at this university. These are precious annals-of-freedom documents. So I shall translate them and we can post them to The New Republic."

"Now hold on a minute," Sam said. "What if--"

"Or maybe The National Enquirer. They must be posted from the branch office near my university. It's more dependable. Or does your foreign affairs department have guangxi with the clerks there?

Pecks at the door were heard.

Sam said, "I better go jack the dean off some more, before Trigger sends him to fetch the Public Security Bureau."

"No," said Mustapha. "Jacking off time is finished. We will search this place after you have burned something." A glance at Polly brought forth a slight smile.

"Yes, Sammy," she said. "You've got to burn something made of paper."

Polly reached under the bed and produced a complete, unabridged, thirty five-cent Pocket Book Special 1946 edition of Dr. Spock. It was something she had found under a pile of rotting blue stencils in a corner of the so called library. It had evidently been a missionary's copy, inscribed with various religious citations and dedications, perhaps used to rear a child of God who was to be expelled by the Chi-coms Before he/she could learn to forget Daddy's identity at the age of four months, as the doctor predicts in an early chapter. It was the edition where all babies are referred to with the masculine pronoun, and only Daddy works, and the doctor will come to your house the moment the baby's stool liquifies. The cover was hanging loose, but the volume itself was solid. It had survived Liberation, the Anti-Rightist Campaign, the Three Red Flags Movement, the Cultural Revolution, the Struggle to Combat Spiritual Pollution, and it made an admirable bonfire in the bathtub.

"It looks all wrong," said Mustapha. "They'll never believe this is the proper set of ashes." He stirred them with his toe.

Polly said, "Of course, you're aware that they'll tear this place to pieces the minute we all go down to the cafeteria for lunch."

"How about our jade chop?" asked Sam. "We might put strips of paper across the door, glue them into place, seal them in red ink with our jade chop and--"

"Are you willing to perform this ritual every time you step across the threshold?" said Mustapha. "And do you really suppose a few pieces of rice paper would deter these men who took this town away from the Japanese, Chiang Kai Shek and the Americans one-two-three? No, not only must we find the essays, but we must cleanse this flat of very piece of paper in it. Your Chinese friends' lives are forfeit if their names appear anywhere in this room."

Mustapha almost leapt in his glee at the grandeur of his own suggestion. "Yes," he said, "give everything to the xiao har. She'll eat them. But first, you must let the old teacher and the spy into your bathroom and display the ashes to them. Chagrin them. Mention academic freedom and righteousness."

They gathered around to primp Sam up a bit before he fetched the commies in.

"Give those terrible men a moving speech," said Mustapha. "Mention Abraham Lincoln."

"Lu Xun," said Polly.

"Yes, for sure Lu Xun. And Joan of Arc."

"Baba," said the baby through a mouthful of paper. Chinese for Daddy.

Then, almost cackling, Mustapha pushed Sam to the door, unlatched it for him and herded the woman and child to hide in the kitchen.

Rong could be heard whispering something hopeless in Chinese about returning at a more convenient time. Sam opened the door and said, "Careful, Professor. You may get yourself Hu You Banged."

"I beg your pardon?"

"Send the boy away and we'll discuss this seriously."

A plea for pity welled up in his ancient eyes. "I cannot," he said. Obviously he couldn't discuss the nature of his relationship with Trigger, so he started in on his spiel again, from the top.

Sam had listened to this on occasions as innocuous as dinner invitations. But this time, though the words were verbatim, the delivery was different--pure terror, like an animal's. More was at stake here than just his apartment on the fifth floor where the rats were a little less dense. Rong knew first-hand what "the leaders" were capable of. The adolescent fury of the Red Guards had merely been a surgical instrument in their hands.

Sam had to look away.

He saw Trigger now. Distinguished only by an extra-tough pair of buttocks, able to withstand extra hours of hard-bench political study meetings, this boy exerted the power of terror over a venerated scholar. Sam was frightened by totalitarian instincts in such a young man. What would he be like when the cynicism of middle age set in, if he was already "betraying to the authorities"? Prepare a post in Beijing; someone is on his way.

"Welcome, Trigger," said Sam. "I have something to warm you up. Won't you come peek in my bathtub? Notice the label on the porcelain: Victory Brand. Does that ring a bell in a postgraduate's little brain? It should. Answer carefully now."

"You have burned nothing," said Trigger. "The papers are concealed somewhere." He spoke in Chinese. This informant planted among the English majors couldn't cough up enough English to express such a complex notion.

"What kind of fucking grade do you expect to get off me?" Sam screamed down into his face. "How about I give you a makeup exam right now? Define crimethink. Identify Big Brother. You little puke, I--"

Something exploded like gunpowder in Trigger's eyes. Though his body kept still, his mouth silent, Trigger's eyes spoke to Sam, and they said, "I know you social-climbing aesthetes. China had plenty of you before Liberation. All I have to do is write two consecutive, parsable sentences and you'll give me at least a B-plus. These ashes mean nothing to you, San Mu Lao Shi. You gorge yourself on Chinese rice, and you puff up your vita with Chinese publications to bring the personal fame which the declining bourgeoisie crave as a substitute for the self-respect that capitalism fails to provide. You assume that soon you'll return to your country and lay your head down in peace. But we have to stay here and try to keep from smothering each other. This is your forty days in the wilderness. For us it's been forty centuries."

"The leaders will consider this an unfriendly act," said Rong. He somehow managed to storm out of the flat while simultaneously asking Trigger's permission to do so.

Trigger removed his eyes from Sam and quietly followed the old man out the door.

"What does the baby have in her mouth?"

"What doesn't she have in her mouth?"

"It looks as though she has found the papers."

Sam's daughter was on the kitchen floor, selecting mushy fragments from her behind-the-fridge stash of subversive documents and doling them out to Sam's wife and pal, who squatted in an adoring semicircle before her.

Polly gave Sam a couple of handfuls and said, "Those students trusted you with their words. You have honor."

It was the first time that possibility had occurred to him.

They all sat down to read the curiously tight, controlled hands:

We are finished with the ten years' chaos. We are modernizing now, and the people don't need to hear bad news....

The workers are not involved and the students are nothing without them. So foreign experts need not write home saying that our society is unstable....

A foreigner, especially an American, can never understand what Lu Xun meant when he said, "In China, men eat each other." If we take a look at the way men are behaving today in the new free markets, we will see why we must move more slowly, why we are still unfit for democracy....

The younger students are just bored. They think that democracy is disco dancing and brawls in the lunch lines. This is nothing....

Mustapha lay down on the bamboo mats to sleep, cursing under his breath. Polly fixed instant noodles.

Sam and the baby made lots of spitballs.

Ax-Honey

Shades of the prison-house begin to close
Upon the growing boy.
*--*Wordsworth, *Intimations of Immortality*

Giant Biff sure liked Axelrad. Always had, ever since prep school, when the big boys had raided "Axle-grease's" sanity daily for four years: ruining his shirts and books with a carefully-proportioned mixture of fire extinguisher chemicals and fountain pen ink; full-pressing him high over their heads by the lapels of his uniform blazer so the girls would laugh at him; in general, just seeing how many new and different ways they could elicit the famous Look from his cherubic kisser.

Hunched double, his shoulders rounded, his eyes lit up a yield-sign yellow, staring out into mid-distances, his entire compact organism trembling in fear and ecstasy, teensy boy Axelrad would get this Look when the bullies at prep school wreaked "death and skunion" upon his head. He was little and lived in terror and everybody assumed, for some odd reason, that he loved it.

The two of them wound up in the same boys' camps, of course, summer after summer, where they observed but did not participate in the kind of homoerotic nude gang romps that traditionally take place on horseback and lake shores all across North America, under the auspices of not-so-latent camp counselors. They observed but did not participate in the obligatory gang fights with the local hayseeds where at least one boy customarily had to lose at least one eye or testicle to effect the redemption of the camp's regional reputation for masculinity.

There'd been many slow river runs where Biff and Ax-honey wound up having to share a two-man raft with each other and several hundred leeches. And always, as the sun sank down behind the standard cathedral of pines, young Biffy would get overexcited, cut himself a willow switch, and chase his whipping boy around camp, trying to conjure up the Look in his beautiful face once again. As the summers drew to a close and inevitable, miserable, humiliating, tortured prep school days beckoned, Axelrad would let himself and his fleet buttocks be caught and chastised more frequently.

The summer they finally grew out of camp, one or the other of their dads got a temporary something-or-other in Hawaii or Florida or someplace like that with an ocean. And, of course, the boy whose dad it was invited the other boy and, obviously, they both threw tantrums and feigned apoplexy until their respective sets of parents okayed the deal. As much as they loathed each other, they had become inseparable.

They spent the summer hanging around this awful older person who, ten years earlier in American history, would've fed them sordid candies, but now supplied them with stacks of literature whose politics Axelrad ignored and Biff misunderstood. They spent their mornings pamphleteering fat flowered tourists on the sunny back patios of Hawaiian (or Floridian) beach-front hotels, and when Security came, Biff and Axelrad threw their pamphlets high up in the sea breeze, to scatter for all to read, and they ran.

They had their first dope/ ocean/ sex experience together, snorkeling naked on windowpane acid with or without girls in knit bikinis, the usual thousands of tiny phosphorescent angelfish and seahorses tickling new hairs on tight groins and thighs and scrota. And they spent their afternoons trying to dry out in a neglected papaya grove with a certain wet smell that caused slim boners to slap against flat young guts; and Biff would curl back his lip and try to elicit the Look from Axelrad again, but only with cruel words now, no willow switch, for repressed adulthood loomed on the watery horizon.

This singular relationship continued up to grad school, when they'd each flown away over the Rocky Mountains, unambitious Biff typically to poop out and drop to earth sooner than lithe, well-connected Axelrad. But, whenever he needed distance from his death-in-life at Kanorado A&M, Biff cut classes and drove up to the glamorous University of Chicago to be reunited once again with his little buddy from way-back.

The humidity turned out to be roughly the same up north as in Kanorado, so Biff's expanding forehead was permanently damp as he and Axelrad took part in a whole rigmarole of complex and expensive Illinoisan depravity. These were the sorts of extravagances that can only take place in huge cities among no-longer-young leftwing types, the largest of whom has recently extorted one good student loan. They were the disorienting sorts of extravagances where, in an advanced form of the game of "chicken," you pay a homosexual gigolo to come sodomize you and your pals.

Well, Biff and Axelrad didn't actually take part in that particular depravity. But they did chip in a good part of the student loan so they could look at the bought homo and talk to him while their Illionoisan friends all lined up, ready to stick scrawny butts up in the air, to see who would be brave enough to panic and snap his cheeks shut last.

That was very icky, almost unmentionably icky. But there was an elemental beauty in its sheer advancedness. One must admit that it would be difficult to devise a more advanced game of "chicken." Besides, Biff wanted to be a writer one day, and he naturally projected his pipe-dream upon bookish Axelrad, and he knew it was high time the two of them started accumulating the kind of true-to-life personal experiences that alone interest Gulf and Western's novelizing subsidiaries.

So everybody got out of his head and wound up in a moiling circle with or without total strangers of various genders, exchanging intensely affectionate or hateful blows or caresses, and not one intelligible word was uttered for hours on end. Aborigine time, buffalo time, gland time.

And they would chew on all the various cacti and fungi whose so-called psychomimetic effects Axelrad would dismiss, even while stuffing his mouth and floating off his couch, as "nothing more than glorified dizziness."

"Come on, Axhole," Biff would feel his mouth say, independent of his will, as he tried to count the green snakes forming around the necks of everyone in the room. "You're not gonna have a chromosome left in your whole body come morning. So you might's well enjoy it. Tell yourself you're seeing God, or boy-sized hot-dogs parading around in little britches or something."

And, of course, Biff found no distance doing any of these things in Illinois, no distance from Kanorado or himself. Wise men, Emerson and Modigliani (the painter, not the economist prick), tell us that travel is a "fool's paradise" and a mere "substitute for work." Biff was finding this to be true. He was left with nothing to show for these trips but the conviction that he must start swimming laps daily at Kanorado A & M's multi-billion-dollar athletic complex. (KA & M couldn't afford to re-bind the Chaucer concordance in the library, so bench-presses were out.) Also, he must start sedulously taking normal women out on dates. Pull himself together, act regular for once.

Because, after all, a strict regimen of carousing with just other boys in big cities, broken up only intermittently by sexless sojourns of freshman composition teaching on the Great Plains, can lead to emotional regression and, yes, homosexuality. And there's nothing more ridiculous-looking than a seven-foot cock queen, pudgy to boot.

Biff feared nothing more than the irreversible process of

emotional regression. He could still remember the chills that shot through his skull when he saw that publicity shot of John Lennon, eyes closed, his body curled bare-naked like a foetus around Ono, who was fully clothed and staring directly at the camera in hideous cannibal triumph. Total regression that was, on the part of the author of "I am the Walrus." What comes before the in-utero state? Nothing. That particular Beatle was begging to be annihilated; that haole kid's timing couldn't have been better.

Now, how would such a thing look in Biff's case? Especially grotesque. For such a healthy-sized man to curl foetally around such a petite, even diminutive creature as the female of the species--well, his husky shinbone alone would obliterate her from view (whoever she was), from the shank of her knee to the bridge of her no doubt sweet button nose. It would be too silly.

Still, though he didn't know why, Biff kept going on these long bye-byes, showing up uninvited in Axelrad's kitchen with a long accordion of federally insured fifty dollar bills stapled end to end.

"Ax-honey, I'm talking fancy bucks," he'd yell, flinging and unfurling green party streamers all around the room. And, though Axelrad was too sophisticated to dive for the dough, he did treat his huge house guest right from that moment on, and let him sleep, when sleep came, in the middle of his homoerotic bedroom floor.

In wee-hour sleep talk, the giant would tell the dwarf that this was just one last fling before the Republicans and the fascists exterminated them and the other intellectuals.

About the Author

When Tom Bradley was a little boy he was given a gazetteer for Christmas. As little boys will, he looked up all the places in the world that start with the F-word. There were two, Fukien in China and Fukuoka in Japan. Little did he suspect that he would one day be exiled to both.

Tom is a former lounge harpist. During his pre-exilic period, he played his own transcriptions of Bach and Debussy in a Salt Lake City synagogue that had been transformed into a pricey watering hole by a nephew of the Shah of Iran.

He taught British and American literature to Chinese graduate students in the years leading up to the Tiananmen Square massacre. He was politely invited to leave China after burning a batch of student essays about the democracy movement rather than surrendering them to "the leaders."

He wound up teaching conversational skills to freshman dentistry majors in the Japanese "imperial university" where they used to vivisect our bomber pilots and serve their livers raw at festive banquets. But his writing somehow sustains him.

His books include; *Vital Fluid, Even the Dog Won't Touch Me, Put It Down in a Book, Hemorrhaging Slave of an Obese Eunuch,* and the Sam Edwine pentateuch.

"Tom Bradley is one of the most exasperating, offensive, pleasurable, and brilliant writers I know. I recommend his work to anyone with spiritual fortitude and a taste for something so strange that it might well be genius."

Denis Dutton, *Arts & Letters Daily*

www.ingramcontent.com/pod-product-compliance
Lightning Source LLC
Chambersburg PA
CBHW030147200626
46812CB00015B/1730